Praise for

JESSICA STEELE:

Jessica Steele has written over seventy-five books for Harlequin Romance® and continues to be loved by readers around the world!

"Jessica Steele pens an unforgettable tale."
—*Romantic Times*

"Jessica Steele dishes up witty dialogue and engaging scenes to energize her pleasing tale."
—*Romantic Times*

"Jessica Steele's [stories are] delightfully packed with emotions and warm, tender characters."
—*Romantic Times*

Jessica Steele lives in a friendly Worcestershire village with her super husband, Peter. They are owned by a gorgeous Staffordshire bull terrier called Florence, who is boisterous and manic, but also adorable. It was Peter who first prompted Jessica to try writing and, after her first rejection, encouraged her to keep on trying. Luckily, with the exception of Uruguay, she has so far managed to research inside all the countries in which she has set her books—traveling to places as far apart as Siberia and Egypt. Her thanks go to Peter for his help and encouragement.

Books by Jessica Steele

HARLEQUIN ROMANCE®

3763—A PAPER MARRIAGE
3741—AN ACCIDENTAL ENGAGEMENT
3721—A PROFESSIONAL MARRIAGE
3695—HIS PRETEND MISTRESS

HER BOSS'S MARRIAGE AGENDA

Jessica Steele

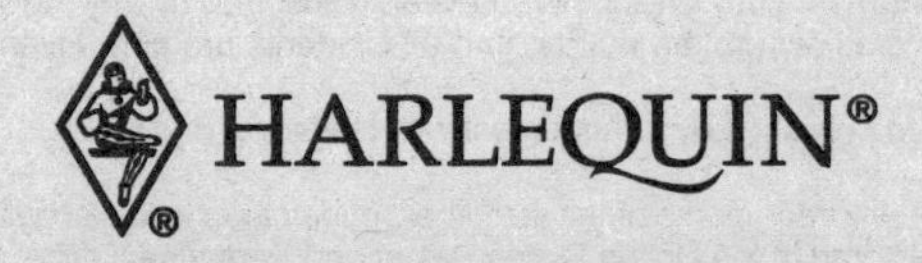

TORONTO • NEW YORK • LONDON
AMSTERDAM • PARIS • SYDNEY • HAMBURG
STOCKHOLM • ATHENS • TOKYO • MILAN • MADRID
PRAGUE • WARSAW • BUDAPEST • AUCKLAND

ISBN 0-373-03787-2

HER BOSS'S MARRIAGE AGENDA

First North American Publication 2004.

This edition published by arrangement with Harlequin Books S.A.

Visit us at www.eHarlequin.com

Printed in U.S.A.

CHAPTER ONE

ERIN was in the habit of waking early. Dawn was just breaking on that Monday when she awoke, and while knowing she would not go back to sleep again she let her thoughts drift.

She was getting used to living and working in London now, albeit that her job was only temporary. A month ago she had been living in the tiny village of Croom Babbington, with her father, in the house she had lived in all her life.

Her parents had divorced when she had been five years old, her mother declaring she'd had enough of domesticity. She had walked out of their Gloucestershire home. That her mother had soon fallen into the domesticity trap and married again shortly after her divorce was neither here nor there—two years later Nina, as she preferred Erin to call her, had walked out of that marriage too. 'Never again!' she had vowed.

Nina had stuck to it too. Though that had not precluded her from having a string of admirers. Erin thought of her with love and affection. Nina had not abandoned her entirely, but, now living in Berkshire, she would make a point of coming to see her every two or three months. Erin did not go to Berkshire to visit with her mother. For one thing, Erin's father would not allow it.

Unbelievably he was still coldly bitter, seventeen years later, that the woman he had married had walked out on him and he did not want his daughter growing up 'wild' like her mother. For another thing, while Erin knew there was a bond of love between her and Nina, her vain mother had no intention of anyone in her circle knowing that she had a daughter. Particularly when as Erin had grown up she had blossomed into a blonde-haired, violet-eyed, something of a beauty too. Erin had learned not to mind that her mother did not want her to visit, though life was never dull when Nina was around.

However, it was probably because life with her strict father was a touch repressing that she had started to think that surely there should be more to life than getting up in the morning and going to a dull going-nowhere secretarial job. Erin had immediately felt guilty for that thought, because he had been a wonderful father, always there to comfort and counsel.

It had been his idea some years previously that she undertake a course of business studies combined with secretarial training. He had suggested it after one Sunday when her mother had breezed in, kissed his cheek regardless that he froze at such contact, and blithely told him, 'I'm taking Erin out to lunch. You don't mind?' she'd asked as an afterthought.

That night he had suggested that there would always be work for personal assistants. While financially there was no need for her to work—he had inherited wealth which he added to by shrewdly dealing in stocks and shares—it would, he'd said with a smile, keep her out of mischief.

Erin had trained hard, worked well, and found her first job exceedingly boring. Six months ago she had changed jobs and gone to work for Mark Prentice.

She could not have said she found that job any more scintillating than the job she had left, but when she had been working for Mark for a couple of months life had suddenly started to pick up. Mark had asked her out. She had thought he was seeing someone else, but she had obviously got that wrong.

She'd dated before, but her father always insisted that any male friend should come to the house to call for her. Which meant that while they were given a grilling before being allowed to take her out, Erin was given a grilling when she arrived back home—her strict father wanting to know in detail everything that had gone on.

She knew that her father loved her, and that he was still afraid she might turn out 'wild'. But, while it was true she had inherited some of her mother's genes, she had also inherited some of his too. And while she might feel a healthy interest in experimenting, Erin had no intention of losing her virginity to just anybody.

Mark had been happy enough to call at the house for her, but not so happy when, returning her home, her father had been up waiting, with no intention of going to bed until her escort had departed. Nor, Mark had found out, was Erin interested in staying overnight at his place.

Her romance with Mark Prentice, Erin had discovered, was not to last long. She had still been working for Mark six weeks ago. She had not seen him the previous evening, and had been busy beavering away when Dawn Mason, an ex-girlfriend of his, had sauntered into her office with the tie he had worn the day before dangling from her fingers.

'I'll just take this through to Mark,' she'd said, adding archly, 'He left it at my place last night.'

Erin was so stunned she didn't say a word—then. She did ten minutes later, though, when, clearly having let Dawn out through his other door, Mark came in to see Erin.

'Did you stay at Dawn Mason's place last night?' Erin asked directly—fully expecting him to deny it.

'I—um—yes,' he had the decency to admit.

'You—didn't...?' She couldn't finish it.

'Well, *you* wouldn't!' he returned defensively.

And that was when Erin discovered that she was neither her father nor her mother, but a person in her own right—and not the rather quiet mouse she had sometimes suspected she might be.

Without more ado she got up from her chair, picked up her jacket and shoulder bag, and told Mark Prentice, 'Perhaps Dawn Mason would like to do your typing for you as well,' and walked out of her job.

She did not regret her decision to leave her job, and in fact felt quite proud of that spurt of spirit that had decreed she wasn't going to meekly sit there and take any sort of nonsense.

A week later, however, and she was starting to feel that life was just a tiny bit dull. She had an allowance from her father, so did not need to work, but she applied for other jobs, and could not help feeling that other young women of her age must be having a much better time than she was having.

A day after that and she was starting to believe that they probably had a much better time because they probably weren't virgins. Well, she decided, she could jolly well do something about that, and would—at the first opportunity!

And then she remembered her father. How could she? How could she possibly? He had always insisted that she be honest with him. So how could she come home and tell him what she'd been up to?

Another two gloomy days passed—and then something happened that was to change her world completely.

She met Charlotte Fisher. There were two large houses on the edge of the village. Erin and her father lived in one of them; Charlotte Fisher and her parents had at one time lived in the other. Charlotte was a few years older than Erin, but the two had liked each other and had got on well. But Charlotte and her family had left the area five or six years ago, so it was a complete surprise for Erin to bump into her at the village post office.

'Charlotte! What are you doing here?' she exclaimed.

'Erin!' Charlotte beamed, and, post office business forgotten, they were soon chatting away as though Charlotte had never left. Charlotte filled in that her parents still lived in Bristol but that she now lived in London and was shortly to be married. 'Gran still lives here, and I've brought Robin to introduce him to her. Can you come and have a coffee with us?' she invited. 'I've only popped out to get Gran some stamps she needed.'

Erin declined the invitation, guessing that Charlotte's grandmother would want Charlotte and her fiancé all to herself for the few hours they would be there. But she and Charlotte ambled to the corner of the street, catching up on each other's news.

'Did you start that business course?' Charlotte asked. 'I remember you were thinking about it around the time the removal vans turned up at our old house.'

Erin nodded. 'Started and finished. I'm between jobs at the moment, though,' she confided.

'What a pity you don't live in London.' Charlotte remarked. 'I could do with some help.'

'And I could do with a change,' Erin commented lightly.

And suddenly Charlotte was taking her up on her comment, telling her that she was in textiles, in a smallish way, and did her own paperwork, but what with the wedding coming up she was so far behind it was a nightmare. 'It would only be temporary, to get me out of the muddle I'm in, but I'd love it if you'd come and help me out! Do say you'll come?' she urged.

And at once Erin felt a rush of excitement at the idea. That excitement mingled with a sense of relief that here was a chance to get away from the utter dullness of her present existence. 'I'd love to,' she answered. She responded enthusiastically—but even as she was speaking she was suddenly swamped by the thought that her father would frown on the notion. Charlotte, too, it seemed, had just remembered him.

'Oh! Your father!' she exclaimed. 'Will he let you come? Is he still vetting everyone you meet and everything you do?'

It came as a bit of a shock to Erin that outsiders were aware of how watchful her father was over her. But at the same time she felt instantly disloyal to him for allowing Charlotte to say such a thing unchecked. But then again this new and spirited person that had sprung to life in her ten days ago was starting to twitch again, that the whole village seemed to think that she could not take a decision unless her father agreed.

'Oh, I'm sure he won't mind,' answered she who had never spent a night anywhere when she wasn't under the same roof as him. She knew in advance that to even think of moving away to London, even if it would be only temporary, was a non-starter. 'But he wouldn't be very happy if I left home to live in a bedsit somewhere.' Erin started to retreat. 'And to rent what he'd consider a decent flat in London would cost the earth. I just couldn't let him pay.'

'I have it!' Charlotte exclaimed. 'And it would be doing us both a favour.' Hurriedly she went on to explain that when she had left her Bristol home for London her father had thought much the same as Erin's father, and so had bought her a tiny mews place. 'It's only very tiny, a small apartment, really, but I've been dithering about what to do about it. I've been unsure about selling it, and I feel a bit nervous about renting it out to someone I don't know. But, Erin, you'd be ideal!'

Erin felt another rush of excitement, the idea beginning to take root. Though she tried for calm as she began to point out, 'You'd want a London rent…'

'No, I wouldn't,' Charlotte denied. 'Just a token rent, if you insist. But you'd be more of a caretaker for me—which would give me space to decide what I want to do with it. It's only poky, compared with the room you're used to, but I fell in love with it straight away and I'm sure you will too. Do say you'll come?'

Already Erin was ninety percent of the way there—Mrs Johns, their housekeeper, had been with them for years and would continue to look after her father. 'If it's so small, will it be big enough for both of us?'

'Oh, I'm seldom there!' Charlotte replied cheerfully. 'To be honest, I spend most of my time at Robin's place. And with the wedding coming nearer and nearer, and my mother panicking we'll never be ready in time, when I'm not at Robin's I'm down in Bristol. Now, do say yes?'

'Er—may I let you know?'

Charlotte at once gave her several phone numbers. 'I know I've rather dropped it on you. It's a surprise to me too.' She grinned. 'But if I'm not at work, or you can't get me on my mobile, ring me on Robin's number—but only if the answer's yes.'

They parted company and Erin, her head full of her meeting with Charlotte, returned home to be greeted by her father, who reminded her that she had not got him the padded envelope she had gone to the post office for.

'I'll go back,' she said. 'I—er—met Charlotte Fisher.'

'Charlotte Fisher? Good heavens! Charlotte Fisher who used to live next door?'

Erin relayed how Charlotte had returned to introduce her fiancé to her grandmother—and the rest of their conversation.

'You told her you'd like to go?' he enquired, not sounding anywhere near as shocked and stern as Erin had anticipated.

'I wouldn't mind. It would only be temporary,' she added hastily. 'I—um—thought you'd be upset.'

'I admit I'm not keen on the idea, but in all truth I expected when you turned twenty that you might soon want to stretch your wings a bit and want to leave home.'

'You did?' Erin was astonished.

'I've done my best to protect you, but I accepted some while ago that I would be unlikely to keep you with me for ever.'

Again Erin was surprised, and touched. 'Oh, Dad,' she said softly.

But that shared moment of empathy was as much as Leslie Tunnicliffe would allow, and he abruptly went on to practicalities. And Erin discovered that he was not yet ready to let go his protection of her when he declared, 'Naturally I shall want to see this mews apartment you're moving into. And of course you'll pay Charlotte Fisher a proper rent—I'll take care of that side of things.'

It was not what Erin wanted. She felt on the brink of gaining her independence and wanted to be self-reliant. But, against that, he was her father and she loved him, and he must be having a hard enough time letting her go, albeit only temporarily.

So she agreed, and found that she did not have to phone Charlotte Fisher because Charlotte phoned her. Not to tell her she'd had second thoughts, as Erin at first feared, but to endorse that she really, really needed her. 'It would be such a tremendous help to me just now if you could free me from that mountain of paperwork,' she pressed.

'When would you like me to start?' Erin answered, and on Charlotte's cry of glee it was settled.

Erin had spent the following day putting together such of her belongings that she would need for what Charlotte vaguely felt would be a three-month arrangement. And, the day after, Leslie Tunnicliffe got into his car and followed his daughter's car to London.

And, as Charlotte had thought, Erin at once fell in love with the mews apartment. It was a first-floor apartment but had its own front door, the rooms being reached by a steep and narrow staircase. Part of the mews flat was over an archway that led into a large cobbled courtyard. On one side of the archway was the bedroom and bathroom, the part over the arch doing service as a dining area with a tiny kitchenette adjoining. This led into an absolutely charming, if small, sitting room. But, more to the point, her father, with the comment that she wouldn't be practising any cat-swinging skills, seemed to approve of her temporary abode too.

'You're a good girl,' he said, when she went to see him off. 'I trust you, Erin, to remember your upbringing.'

Erin, who was about to get her first taste of real freedom, had a feeling that to remember the dos and don'ts of her upbringing might be a bit restricting. But he was her father, she loved him, and did not want him to worry about her.

'I'll try to be good,' she answered lightly, straining at the leash to let go of being good. This, for her, was a big adventure. She had started to crave adventure.

He kissed her goodbye and she returned to the apartment with an involuntary smile breaking across her features as she climbed the narrow staircase. Who would have thought it? Last week life had been deadly dreary and she had been upset at Mark Prentice's behaviour. But look at how exciting life was now! And Mark Prentice? Pfff! Erin realised then that she had never cared very deeply for Mark.

For a moment she felt a touch panicky that she might be a bit more like her mother than she had realised. Her mother, having walked out on two marriages and determined not to venture into a third, had adopted the habit of 'letting them go'—just as if they were in her employ—when any of her men friends mentioned the 'M' word.

Erin grew calm again. She wasn't like her mother in that area; she just knew that she was not. But thinking of her mother made her realise that, with everything happening so fast, she hadn't informed Nina of the latest developments.

Before unpacking, Erin took out her mobile phone and thumbed out Nina's number. Unusually, she was in—and disbelieving.

'Happy Harry actually let you go!' she squealed.

'It's only temporary. For three months or so,' Erin replied. Happy Harry! Her mother was incorrigible.

Nina laughed. 'You won't want to go back after three months! I know I wouldn't! Give me your address. I'll come over and see you when I have a minute.'

Now, Erin stretched in her bed. All that had been a month ago. She had begun working for Charlotte and had soon made inroads into the paperwork. Erin left her bed and headed for the shower. She got ready for the day, fearing that the three months Charlotte had said it would take to sort out her office and get everything up to date was an overestimate. Even if she only went in part time, Erin considered, she would still shortly have everything in apple-pie order.

And the trouble was that once the office was up to date Erin knew she would have to go back home. And—Nina had been right. She did not want to go back to Croom Babbington to live. She had spent the weekend there with her father, returning to London only yesterday; the weekend had seemed to go on for ever. Not that there was a lot happening on her social scene in London. Nina had been to see her, and Charlotte had been to remove the remainder of her clothes. Erin had met Robin, Charlotte's fiancé, a man in his mid-thirties, a non-pushy kind of man whom Erin had taken to straight away.

Robin was totally unlike Gavin Gardner, the slightly pushy man who had the industrial unit next to Charlotte's. Gavin had asked Erin out within the first half an hour of meeting her. But while Erin was quite keen to 'cut her teeth', as it were, she had discovered that there was something inbred in her that ruled out brash males of the Gavin Gardner type. She had refused his invitation. That did not put him off. He continued to ask her out—she continued to refuse.

Erin left the mews apartment to join the rest of the commuting herd. She had soon learned the folly of driving through London in the rush hour to reach her temporary job, and then trying to find a nearby parking spot. Public transport might be crowded, but it was the better option.

She had Fisher Fabrics in her view when Gavin Gardner fell into step with her. 'Good weekend?' he enquired for openers.

Erin saw no reason not to answer him. 'I stayed the weekend in my old home,' she replied. 'How did your weekend go?' she asked in return.

'It would've been better if you'd featured in it,' he returned flirtatiously.

Dream on! 'Busy?' she enquired, meaning his work—he did something with plastic extrusion.

'Not so busy that I can't spare time to have coffee, lunch, dinner with you. You choose?' he offered.

She laughed. Her lovely mouth curved upwards. He was either much too obvious or she was growing a very faint coating of sophistication—she wasn't sure which. At any rate, she was glad that they had just reached Fisher Fabrics. 'Bye, Gavin,' she bade him.

'One day,' he threatened. 'One day.'

Erin was smiling when she entered the building that was more like an overlarge shed than anything else. Charlotte, the first in, looked up and saw her smiling face. 'Gavin Gardner?' she guessed.

'He'll give up eventually.'

'If you believe that you'll believe anything. How's your father?' she asked, aware that Erin returned to her old home every weekend.

'He was pleased to see me.' Her smile faded. 'I think he's missing me,' Erin added.

'He's bound to. You've been his life since your mother left,' Charlotte commented.

That did not make Erin feel any better. 'Do you think I should go back?' she asked worriedly.

'Grief, no!' Charlotte objected. 'Do you want to?'

It was a truth that, much though she loved her father,

and was grateful to him for his nurturing of her, she was loving her brief time in London. She shook her head. 'No,' she answered honestly. 'I don't. Though the way your paperwork's going,' she felt she should mention, 'it isn't going to take me all of three months to get everything running smoothly.'

Charlotte considered what she'd said for a moment, and then replied, 'Even so, even if you won't need that long, there's nothing to stop you staying on, is there?'

'In London, do you mean?' Erin asked, startled. The thought hadn't occurred to her.

'You'd have no trouble in finding another job—and I'd give you the best ever reference. And I still haven't decided what to do about whether or not to sell the mews place.'

'You're saying I could stay on there?'

'Of course. And, should I decide to sell, I'd give you ample notice so you could look around for somewhere decent. What do you say?'

What Erin wanted to say was, yes, yes, yes. But there was her father to consider. 'May I think about it?' she asked, feeling torn in two.

'Of course,' Charlotte said again, and, smiling, 'And if you're not so busy as I thought you'd be, why don't we drop everything and—shop!' Charlotte was positively beaming. 'I've worked my brain to a standstill this weekend. I'm in need of a stiff dose of retail therapy.'

Erin considered the amount of work she had been going to do that day—not colossal by anyone's standards—and decided that to shop was the best idea she'd heard in a long while. 'Lead on!' she encouraged.

Two hours later, with a satisfactory collection of carriers already starting to mount up, they were seated at the window table of a salubrious café, taking a break.

Charlotte had just commented, 'I think I'll go back for that scarf,' when they both became aware of the tall, dark and, Erin had to admit, very good-looking man who had entered and was approaching their table. 'Josh!' Charlotte exclaimed with delight, and as Erin felt a most peculiar sensation in her heart region the man glanced from Charlotte to Erin, and back to Charlotte again.

'I thought it was you,' he said, having plainly seen Charlotte from the window and come in. 'I could do with a coffee. Shall I join you?'

Charlotte was again delighted. 'Of course. Erin and I are taking a breather from the more serious work of life.' He glanced at their carriers as though quite understanding the ways of women. And while Erin was forming the opinion that he very likely *did* understand the ways of women, thoroughly, Charlotte set about making the introductions.

'This is Joshua Salsbury, Robin's best man at our wedding,' she said, and as Erin noted that the good-looking Joshua Salsbury would be about the same mid-thirties age as Robin, Charlotte was saying, 'Erin Tunnicliffe. Erin hails from the same village in Gloucestershire where I originally came from.'

Joshua Salsbury stretched out his right hand to Erin and, feeling oddly glad that she was wearing a favourite trouser suit that particularly became her, Erin shook hands with him. Then Joshua took possession of a spare chair at their table and, magically, a waitress appeared to take his order.

'You've come to London to shop, Erin? Or do you live here?' he enquired as the waitress departed.

'Erin's trained in business and secretarial work and is here answering my SOS because my Everest-high paperwork grew out of control,' Charlotte answered for her.

'But you decided to hit the shops instead?' he commented pleasantly.

'We're having a lovely time,' Erin said with a smile, saw his glance stray very briefly to her curving mouth, and felt all out of her depth suddenly. So much for the faint coating of sophistication she had thought she might have acquired! She was glad when the waitress returned with his coffee. Then Charlotte was remarking that it seemed ages since she and Robin had seen him.

Him—singular? Was there no Mrs Joshua Salsbury? Looking at him, Erin rather thought that from his well-cut business suit, not to mention his looks—leave alone that the man had charm enough to sink a battleship—there would be any number of females queuing up for that distinction.

Joshua Salsbury answered that he had been out of the country for a while, and asked, 'Have you been in town long, Erin?'

'A month,' she replied pleasantly.

'With another two months to go,' Charlotte filled in. 'I've been trying to persuade Erin to stay on after she has my paperwork up to date.'

'You have a place in town?' he turned to Erin to enquire, and Erin, not knowing if it was common knowledge that Charlotte was living at Robin's apartment, hesitated.

'Erin's caretaking my place for me until I decide what to do with it. Sell it or rent it out,' Charlotte came in openly.

And a short while after that Joshua Salsbury glanced to his watch, finished the last of his coffee, wished them more successful shopping and said that he must be on his way. Remarking that he would be in touch with Robin, he paid for his coffee and theirs, and left them sitting there.

Erin wanted to make some comment about him, ask questions about him, but did not want Charlotte to think she was overly interested in him. In truth, though, Erin felt she had never met anyone like Joshua Salsbury. To her mind he had everything, absolutely everything. Successful, obviously. Without question sophisticated. He made the men she had dated seem mere boys.

'You were saying something about going back for that scarf you were undecided about?' she reminded Charlotte instead.

'I think I will. You know how it is. If I don't buy it now, I shall never find what I'm looking for when I want it.'

Erin returned to the mews apartment at the end of an agreeable day's shopping with a few purchases of her own. But she had to admit that her thoughts were not on the new additions to her wardrobe as she put them away, but on the tall, dark-haired, grey-eyed man, the like of whom had never crossed her path before and, sadly, was never likely to again.

Somehow, Erin just did not seem able to get thoughts of Joshua Salsbury out of her head. He would return frequently to interrupt her concentration throughout the rest of that week as she busied herself with various pieces of correspondence or accounting.

She left London on Friday evening to spend the weekend with her father, and owned to feeling mean and treacherous because she wanted to stay on in London. But the idea of finding a permanent job and staying on just would not leave her. Though it was Sunday afternoon before she was able to broach the subject to her father, and then only by recalling how he had stated over a month ago that he had expected she might want to leave home when she turned twenty.

'Would you mind very much if I didn't come back after I've finished my work for Charlotte?' she asked in a sudden rush, the time growing ever closer to when she should start back for London.

Leslie Tunnicliffe looked at her sharply. 'The grass is obviously greener on the London side,' he answered, and, as terrible as she was feeling, Erin just could not say what she knew he was hoping she would say—that it didn't matter and that she would return to Croom Babbington to live. But, 'I'm being unfair,' he relented after a moment. 'You must enjoy living in London or you wouldn't want to stay on. You'd better tell me about your plans.'

Erin drove back to London and could hardly believe she had her father's blessing to stay. She had told him of Charlotte's opinion that she'd have no trouble in finding another job, and had also told him that Charlotte would give her ample time to look for other accommodation should she ultimately decide to sell the mews apartment. Erin had also assured him that she would come home each weekend, on either Fridays or Saturdays.

Charlotte was at her most encouraging when on Monday Erin told her of her intention to look for a job in London. 'That's great!' she exclaimed, adding, 'Purely selfish of me, I know, but apart from anything else I needn't rush to make a decision about the apartment.'

'Would you mind if I started looking for another job now?'

'As long as you don't leave me straight away,'

Charlotte replied lightly. Then calculated, 'Though if you start going for interviews, say, next week, and then tell your future employer that you want to give a clear month's notice here, that would complete your three months with me. Not that I'd hold you to that if you found an absolute gem of a job,' she added swiftly.

Erin purchased an evening paper on her way back to the mews apartment that evening. She scanned it quickly as soon as she got in, but saw nothing that caused her to want at once to get out her writing materials and apply.

She decided to make her meal and then study the situations vacant more leisurely afterwards. Which in effect was what she was doing when the phone in the tiny apartment rang. Erin had been in the habit of using her mobile phone to make any calls, and had not given out Charlotte's phone number to anyone.

Aware the call would be for Charlotte, Erin went over to answer it. 'Hello,' she said pleasantly—and felt instantly all of a jumble inside when she heard who was calling.

'Hello, Erin,' said a firm, well-modulated voice. 'Josh Salsbury.'

'Oh!' she exclaimed, and wanted to die that she had exclaimed anything, and hurriedly forced herself back together again. 'I'm afraid Charlotte's not here just now.'

'Which makes it just as well that I rang hoping to speak with you.'

He wanted to speak with her! Joshua Salsbury, tall, dark, good-looking—she had never forgotten his face—wanted to speak with *her?*

She tried for even a tiny scrap of his sophistication.

'How can I help?' she asked politely—as if a man of his calibre would need help from her in any way!

'I'd like to have a meal with you,' he replied—straight out, just like that! Her legs went weak.

He was asking her for a date! He was... She collapsed onto the nearest chair. Then to her surprise found that the duplicity of the man she had last dated had affected her more than she had realised. Inasmuch as instead of jumping at the chance to go out with Joshua Salsbury—and surely by 'have a meal with you' he wasn't suggesting that they stay in and she cook it?—she first asked, 'You're not married—or anything?'

'Not married,' he replied, and, sounding amused, 'Or anything. Nor have I ever been married. Though I believe that state is quite popular and that some people actually enjoy it.' Erin felt her lips twitch. Quite clearly he was stating up front that he had positively no interest in being married. Quite clearly, too, when he followed up with, 'Dinner—Friday?' he had no time for trivialities either.

Oh, help. Her insides felt as if they belonged to anyone but her. So who was this casual-sounding person who popped out of her mouth to tell him, 'I'll look forward to it'?

'I'll call for you. Seven-thirty,' he said. 'Until then.' And rang off.

Erin sat too paralysed to move for ages afterwards. All memory of what she had been doing when the phone had rung—checking again the situations vacant column—went from her head. Had that really happened? Had Joshua Salsbury really and truly rung her to ask her out on a date? Had she really and truly accepted?

That he had in fact done just that seemed no less real the next day as she busied herself at Fisher Fabrics. She was in a way grateful that Charlotte was busy for most of the day with buyers who had come to see her work. Part of Erin wanted to tell Charlotte about Josh Salsbury's phone call, but another part of her felt too shy to do anything of the sort. Also, Erin felt she must be vastly different from the type of woman he usually escorted to dinner, and did not want Charlotte to confirm as much by so much as a raised eyebrow.

Though perhaps Charlotte knew that he had intended to phone her? He had the phone number, after all, and, since he was calling at the mews apartment on Friday, he must know Charlotte's address. Perhaps Robin had told him the phone number and the address.

All of which was rather getting away from the point of why Erin felt in such a flutter. Joshua Salsbury was an attractive man of the world and she, Erin Tunnicliffe, was drowning in feelings of insecurity. How on earth was she going to be able to eat so much as a crumb? Just thinking of Josh calling for her, of sitting beside him in his car while he drove them to whichever eating establishment he had chosen, was making her stomach churn. What would she be like on Friday?

Erin arrived home from work on Wednesday still coping with mixed emotions whenever she thought of her proposed dinner date with Josh Salsbury—which she did often. She was half inclined to find his phone number and ring and tell him she could not make it after all. Since he had phoned on Monday to make the arrangement for Friday, it wasn't as if he was exactly champing at the bit to go out with her, was it?

On the other hand he was probably a very busy man. The day he had joined her and Charlotte for coffee he had said he had been out of the country for a while. Perhaps he was frequently out of the country. Either that or she had been right first off, Erin mused agitatedly, and he was not in any way eager to see her.

That was when her pride reared up. And, conversely, she was then blessed if she would go out with the wretched man.

She found the piece of paper Charlotte had given her with her contact numbers. But before Erin could ring Robin's number to enquire about Josh Salsbury's number she was recalling how she had come to London to, as it were, get herself a life.

Hadn't she come away from Croom Babbington precisely because life was deadly dull? Hadn't she determined to be like other women? Hadn't she decided to seek a little excitement? And remembering her uneventful father-waiting-up-for-her-when-she-got-in life, a lot of excitement, actually.

So was she to fall at the first hurdle? Yes, but man-about-town, had-it-all Joshua Salsbury? Erin had an idea she would be wading in deep, deep waters way above her head if she went out with him. But then again—she gave herself a mental shake—for goodness' sake, wasn't it high time that she *did* wade into those waters? Even if she did quail a little at the thought of so much as dipping a toe in those waters with Josh Salsbury there as chief swimming instructor.

The next morning Erin told Charlotte about her date for the following evening. 'You're going out with Josh Salsbury!' Charlotte exclaimed, to Erin's relief not raising an eyebrow but smilingly adding, 'You jammy—!' She broke off. 'You *do* know that half the beauties in London are waiting for his phone call?'

'I was as surprised as you…' Erin began, but someone called to see Charlotte and Erin turned her attention back to work—but not her full attention.

Half the beauties in London… Half the *sophisticated* beauties in London, would that be? Again Erin was unsure. The last thing she wanted was that Josh Salsbury should think her stupid or naïve.

On that basis alone, when Charlotte was free Erin asked her for his phone number. Charlotte was kind enough to not ask why she wanted it, and, after checking her personal directory, wrote down both his business and his home number.

By the time Erin went home that evening, however, she had given herself a stern lecture. For goodness' sake, hadn't she wanted more adventure in her life? Buck your ideas up, do. Did she want to see Josh Salsbury again or not?

There was nothing more to think about. She very definitely did. And she would. Though how she was going to feel around seven-twenty-five tomorrow night, while she waited for his ring at the door, she did not want to think.

She decided to have her meal and check through the situations vacant of that evening's paper for a job that would have something about it and that wouldn't leave her bored to tears in a month. Then she would check her wardrobe for something smart, without being over the top, to wear on her date tomorrow.

Erin did not get as far as making a meal. For, on flattening out the paper she had bought on her way home, she was shaken rigid to see a picture of none other than the man she would be dining with the following evening! Pictured with him was an older man, but an equally good-looking man. Both wore dinner jackets, both obviously attending some function or other.

Speedily she scanned the headline. The picture, she read, was of Thomas Salsbury, chairman of Salsbury

Engineering Systems, with his son, Joshua Salsbury, chief executive of the company. The picture had been taken a month earlier, when Thomas Salsbury had been in full health. He had yesterday, unfortunately, been taken ill with a heart attack.

Still feeling somewhat shaken, Erin read it through twice. She learned little more, other than a description of Salsbury Engineering Systems being a huge company of international specialists in complex engineering projects. Globetrotting Joshua Salsbury was expected one day to take over the chairmanship of the company.

Poor Josh, Erin couldn't help thinking. The two men pictured appeared to have a special affinity with each other. As if, without having to broadcast the fact, they cared very much about each other. No way would Josh want to take over the company because of his father's illness. Erin just seemed to know that for a fact.

With all thought of checking the situations vacant columns gone from her mind, she made a cup of coffee, reflecting on her inner turmoil in considering whether or not to cancel her date with Josh, when now it was very likely that he would ring her and suggest postponing it.

Should she ring him? Ring him and say that she'd seen the paper and understood perfectly that he had more pressing matters on his mind than taking her to dinner tomorrow?

Erin did not make that call then, for two reasons. One was that she who had never particularly suffered from shyness in her life suddenly felt incredibly shy. The other reason was that she was pretty certain he was more likely to be at the hospital with his father than at either of the numbers Charlotte had written down for her.

Then her doorbell sounded and Erin went down the stairs to answer it. Only to have thoughts of Josh

Salsbury taken temporarily from her mind when she opened the door and found her mother standing there.

As usual, Nina's standards being of the highest, she looked as smart as ever. 'I was near and realised I'm early for my—appointment. Don't want to appear too eager,' she trilled. 'So I thought I'd come and spend half an hour with my dear daughter.'

'Come up,' Erin invited, wondering how long this present man-friend would last before her mother had to 'let him go'. It was without question that Nina was meeting a male of the species.

Erin led the way to the sitting room and turned, about to ask her mother if she would like some coffee, when she saw that her mother had spotted the evening paper and was staring at it, startled.

'Tommy Salsbury!' she exclaimed, picking up the paper to read what it was all about.

'You know him?' Erin questioned, feeling startled herself.

'I was out with him only last week,' Nina replied, going on in alarm as she put the paper back down, 'Good heavens, he could have had a heart attack while I was with him! Thank goodness I let him go in time!'

Feeling stunned, Erin stared at her parent. 'You—let him go?'

'Let him go. Dumped him, I believe the expression is these days. You know how men get after a while. He'd been asking leading questions about my family, the way men do when they're getting serious. I should have let him go then, at that first sign, but…'

'Serious? As in wedding bells?' Erin asked, her head all of a whirl at this development.

'Serious as in marriage. As in pipe and slippers! As in Boredom County!' At one time Erin might have been amused by Nina, but this wasn't funny. 'He asked me to marry him—I couldn't have that,' Nina stated thoughtlessly.

'You turned him down?'

'Naturally I turned him down!' Nina replied, as if doubting why her daughter should need to ask.

Erin was speechless. For heaven's sake, her mother had been out with the man only last week! Why—Nina 'letting him go' might even have contributed in some large degree to him suffering that heart attack!

'I should have recognised that the writing was on the wall when he introduced his son to me and then started to hint that he wouldn't mind meeting some of my family. But Tommy had always been such good fun that I at first missed the warning signs...'

Her mother had met Joshua Salsbury! Oh, heavens, this was a nightmare! 'You—er—told Mr Salsbury you had a daughter?' Erin asked, and knew she must be in some kind of shock to have asked such a ridiculous question.

'Are you mad?' her mother retorted. 'Of course I didn't. Nor would I consider introducing you to any of my—friends.' But, taking any sting out of those words, she smiled becomingly at her daughter and complimented her, 'You're much too pretty.' And while Erin stared at her beautiful mother, who would always be beautiful, Nina Woodward was going on to amaze her by saying, 'I've been thinking of having some cosmetic surgery.'

'You're having a face lift?' Erin asked, feeling absolutely shattered.

'Must you be so crude?' her mother complained. 'I said I was only thinking of it, so I very probably won't. I wouldn't mind the end result, but I wouldn't care for an anaesthetic—and I certainly wouldn't want it done while I was conscious.'

'Mother, you're beautiful just as you are!' Erin quickly told her, finding the idea of her vain mother going to such lengths frightening, particularly when it was so not necessary.

'You think so?' Nina responded, and appeared to be a little comforted. 'For that I shall forgive you the "Mother" word. Now, if I can just use your bathroom to freshen up, I'll be on my way.'

Erin sat for a long while after her mother had left, going over and over everything in her head. Though in actual fact she knew then, as she had more or less known at once, what she must do.

She had all along been a little trepidatious about her dinner date with Josh Salsbury tomorrow. She had also been excited and eager about it too. Many times she had thought of contacting him to cancel, but the excited and eagerness part had won over the trepidatious part. But now how could she go out with him?

He had met her mother. He in all probability knew that his father had asked her mother to marry him. Just as with that same probability Josh knew that her mother had dumped his parent the moment that proposal was aired, and how her callousness, for that was the way he would most likely see it, had contributed largely to his father being rushed into hospital yesterday. Now, was Joshua Salsbury remotely likely to want to take out to dinner the daughter of the woman who had a big part in causing his father's suffering?

Erin remembered the charming and pleasant dark-haired man who had joined her and Charlotte that morning for coffee. She remembered his firm jaw, his grey eyes which, though friendly then, she did not doubt would turn hostilely cold should she explain who she was. The question of would he want to wine and dine her did not need to be asked. She already knew the answer. He would not.

Erin felt sick inside as she accepted that there was nothing she could do other than telephone him. It was ingrained in her to tell the truth at all times, yet how could she tell him that she was Nina Woodward's daughter? While it was without question that he would be fiercely loyal to his father—it was all there in that newspaper photograph of the two standing together—Erin too felt a loyalty to her parent, no matter what she had or had not done. No way, Erin felt, would she be able to stay quiet while Joshua Salsbury gave forth with some detrimental opinion of her mother.

It was nine-thirty before Erin had herself sufficiently together to pick up the phone and make the call that had to be made. She hoped he would be in. After being in a mental stew over the last few hours, she now wanted it all over and done with. She glanced at her watch again, calculated that if Joshua Salisbury had been hospital-visiting he should be home by now—and dialled. Her call went unanswered.

She rang again a half-hour later. The phone rang out a few times, and when Erin didn't know whether to feel glad or sorry that he still wasn't in, suddenly the ringing tone stopped. 'Salsbury,' said a firm all-male voice.

'Oh, Josh—ua.' She added the last two syllables, realising that they weren't on shortened name terms. 'It's Erin Tunnicliffe.' There was a pause during which he said nothing but waited for her to continue. 'I read in the paper about your father,' she plunged in, in a rush. 'I do hope he is feeling better.'

'Thank you for your concern. He's being well looked after,' Joshua Salsbury replied evenly.

That seemed to end the conversation right there, and Erin realised that about matters close to home, as it were, Josh Salsbury was a very private man. 'The thing is,' she went on in another rush, 'I'm sorry I can't see you tomorrow after all.'

What she had expected, she rather supposed, was some polite, Thank you for letting me know, before he put the phone down. A little to her surprise, though, what she got was a querying, 'You can't?'

Oh, help. Erin thought that perhaps she did owe him some sort of explanation, but if either of them was to use the excuse of his father's illness then Josh had prior claim. She hadn't thought he would bother with wanting to know why, and just wasn't ready. She hurriedly searched round for some truthful excuse—there wasn't one. Not one she could tell him anyway.

'I've—um—there are... That is...' She took a deep breath in an effort to calm down, then continued, 'That is, I've a few complications at the—er—moment.' She felt hot all over, and hoped he would leave it there.

Thankfully, he did, his voice sounding cool and not the least tiny bit disappointed when, not deigning to press her for more, he drawled, 'Why not give me a ring when you have your complications sorted?'

Like he was desperate to see her! 'I...' she began, but he had put down the phone. Well, what had she expected? All too clearly he didn't give a tinker's cuss if he never heard from her again.

And that saddened her. She had liked him. But she didn't have to be the sharpest knife in the drawer to know that she had blown any chance of a second invitation from him. For certain Joshua Salsbury was just not used to women cancelling dinner dates with him.

Just as she knew, circumstances being what they were, that she could never ring him again, Erin also knew he would not be holding his breath waiting for her call. She seemed to know he was not the kind of man who asked twice—and she, Erin knew too, had just blown all chance of ever seeing him again.

CHAPTER TWO

LIFE seemed dull again as Erin journeyed to her place of work the next morning. She wondered about Joshua Salsbury's father and felt sad. She hoped Mr Salsbury would soon be well again. She thought of Joshua Salsbury himself and felt even more depressed. She had ended something before it had begun.

While she accepted that it was most unlikely that her date with him would have gone very far, or even have led to a second date, she didn't so much as have one date with him now.

'Good morning, Erin!' Charlotte greeted her cheerfully as she went in, and was in a chatty mood.

Erin responded as cheerfully as she could manage. After all, it wasn't Charlotte's fault that life had gone back to being as dreary as if she still lived in Croom Babbington.

Erin was amazed that just cancelling a date with a man she hardly knew should so put her spirits at basement level. She hadn't been sure about going out with him anyway, for goodness' sake!

She determined to put 'ring when you have your complications sorted' Joshua Salsbury out of her head. It was for certain he wasn't wasting a second of his day in thinking of her.

But so much for not thinking of him. She had just made some coffee, and Charlotte had joined her for a break, when Charlotte remembered, 'Oh—it's tonight you're going out with Josh Salsbury, isn't it?'

Oh, crumbs. Erin had no idea how friendly Charlotte was with Josh. But since he was to be her fiancé's best man he must be good friends with Robin, and, it was a fair bet, a friend to Charlotte too. Erin knew then that she could not be as open with Charlotte as she would prefer to be—notwithstanding that Erin felt she owed her mother her first loyalty.

'It's—um—off,' she answered, searching for some good reason.

Then Erin discovered that she did not need to search, because Charlotte had either seen the same newspaper or had heard of Thomas Salsbury's heart attack from another source. 'Oh, yes. Josh's father,' she said, and Erin went back to feeling totally fed-up again.

So much so that on her way back to Fisher Fabrics, after going out at lunchtime for something to eat, when Gavin Gardner fell into step with her and asked her to go and have a drink with him that night, she thought, why not?

'You will!' he exclaimed eagerly. 'Great!' And while Erin was already starting to have second thoughts—was her life really that dull?—he was going on, 'I've already had a few jars this lunchtime, to celebrate a business deal I clinched this morning. But we'll celebrate for real tonight. I'll call for you in a taxi. Don't want to risk my driving licence,' he laughed.

Oh, grief, he sounded three parts towards being tipsy before he had another drink. But he had the whole afternoon in which to sober up, and anyway dull was dull, and a drink with a three-quarters-inebriated Gavin, while not putting a shine on her lot, couldn't make it any duller. Live a little, for goodness' sake.

On that thought she gave him her address, and when he suggested seven-thirty she had no trouble in recalling that Josh Salsbury had been going to call for her at seven-thirty that night. 'Make it eight,' she told Gavin as they reached Fisher Fabrics.

'Can't wait,' he answered, and with a too-familiar kind of squeeze to her arm they parted.

Erin knew that she had made a mistake in agreeing to go out with him, but had inherited part of her father's stubborn nature. And even though she knew that what she should do was go next door and tell Gavin Gardner that she had changed her mind, she would not.

She had agreed to go out with him and she would. She had come to London determined to see and experience something of life. But what life would she see or experience if she stayed home the whole of the time—delightful though the mews apartment was?

Erin showered when she got home, while impressing on herself the whole time her need to see and experience life. She selected a deep blue trouser suit from her wardrobe, but was aware that had she been going out with Josh Salsbury she would most likely have chosen a dress—oh, stop thinking about him do. You aren't going out with him; you're going out with Gavin. Get a life! See a bit of life!

Gavin arrived at seven-forty-five. Erin was glad she was ready. Somehow, for all her self-lecture about getting a life, she did not fancy inviting Gavin up to the close confines of the small apartment.

A decision that she knew was the right one when, ogling her figure and her long length of leg in the deep blue trousers, Gavin seemed even more forward than she had thought. To her surprise, though, the pub he took her to was more of a select kind of small hotel with a public bar.

'What are you having?' he asked, and caused her not

to know whether to laugh or be frosty when, looking deeply into her violet eyes, he actually licked his lips.

She decided on humour. 'Just a tonic water, please,' she answered, suspecting he'd done some more celebrating since they had parted at lunchtime and musing it might be a good idea if one of them stayed sober.

So much for him asking what she wanted. 'I put a gin in it,' he informed her when he came back with a couple of glasses in his hands.

Erin could have got cross. But the mere fact he had not tried to conceal what he had done, but had so openly told her, made her feel less irritated than she might have otherwise. She raised her glass to him. 'Congratulations on the deal you made today,' she said in friendly fashion, and smiled.

She was not smiling an hour later, however. Gavin was turning out to be a pain. He had been up to the bar several times to get himself another drink. True, he had bought her one each time—she had three untouched ones lined up in front of her, and that was how they were going to stay: untouched. But he was decidedly the worse for wear.

'Drink up, Erin, you're very slow,' he urged, sounding like a man who was trying hard to pretend he hadn't been staggering the last time he'd returned from the bar.

'No, thanks.' And because this wasn't what she'd had in mind when she'd thought of getting a life, of living a little—she'd rather stay home, thank you very much—'I'll get us a taxi, shall I?' she offered. He'd be falling over his feet if she asked him to go and get one!

Gavin looked at his half-finished drink, then at the beautiful violet-eyed blonde sitting next to him, and positively, if beerily, beamed, 'Splen… good idea. Shall we go straight to your place?'

Oh, dear. He clearly had ideas that she did not have. 'Do you remember where you live?' she asked.

'You want us to go there?'

No, I want to go home and to be able to tell the taxi driver where to take you. Erin might have told him as much, but all at once she felt the grip of his hand as he familiarly decided to make his acquaintance with her thigh.

She might have laughed, but ice entered her soul. This was no laughing matter. Particularly not in a public place, where anybody watching could get totally the wrong idea.

Very firmly she picked up his hand and removed it from her person, and told him coldly, 'You do that again and I shall smack you.'

His face fell at her cross look, and, more than ever wishing she had never agreed to go out with him, Erin turned her head away—and as everything in her jangled from shock, she wished that the ground would open up and take her. For as her eyes focused on the bar so she saw a tall, dark-haired man who was half turned and was watching her and her companion. Oh, *no!* The fates just wouldn't be that unkind!

But they were! There, very obviously getting totally the wrong idea about her and the man she was with, was none other than Joshua Salsbury!

No. Oh, no, her brain screamed. She couldn't believe it. Even as her face flamed—he could not possibly have missed Gavin's familiarity with her thigh—she could not believe it, did not want to believe it. But it was true.

She wanted to look away, but felt hypnotised by a pair of grey eyes that seemed to refuse to let her look away. Oh, grief. She had given up her date with a good-looking man who was totally in charge—for the drunken specimen by her side! Oh, the ignominy of it!

She managed at last to drag her eyes away from Josh Salsbury, and her brain ran off at a tangent. She was still busy coping with her shock at seeing him there, of all places, but she vaguely remembered spotting a private clinic type of place close by. She realised then that Josh had in all likelihood stopped by for a quick drink after visiting his father.

But she had no time for further speculation because Gavin Gardner—who, having sunk the rest of his pint was now too far gone to know when his advances weren't welcome—was again showing some fascination with her thigh.

She couldn't cope, Erin realised. Without so much as a glance in Josh Salsbury's direction she got abruptly to her feet. Gavin got rockily to his feet too, and as he stood there swaying Erin knew that she just couldn't abandon the idiot, much though she would like to.

'Come on,' she said, taking a hold of his arm. He smiled inanely. She didn't think he would be much more trouble. Nor was he, particularly, though it was a shame that they had to walk near the bar, and straight in front of Joshua Salsbury. A shame too that Gavin Gardner's feet should choose that moment to do a wobbly dinky side-step—which brought him stumbling up against the man at the bar.

Josh's hand came out to firmly prop him up. Though it was not to her escort that he addressed his remark but to her when, mockingly, he commented, 'What a one you are for complications, Erin.'

She looked at him, wished that she could think up something sharp and witty with which to reply, but her sharp and witty cupboard was bare. She did the next best thing and ignored him, concentrating instead on getting Gavin out of there before he crashed into anybody else.

'Ooh!' Gavin mumbled when the fresh air hit him, but thankfully his suddenly spinning head cooled any amorous intent he might have previously set his mind on.

Taxis were like buses, Erin fretted. None at all, or three at once. Eventually one came along, and she helped Gavin inside, giving the taxi driver her address. Whereupon Gavin went sleepy and she had to prise him awake in order to extract his address from him.

As the taxi pulled up at her mews address Erin relayed to the driver where Gavin lived. Her idea to pay the driver her fare with a little extra, and then pay him to take Gavin home—while making a note never to go out with him again—became a non-starter. Because as she opened the door and got out, and handed over her fare, Gavin got out too, and the cabbie—clearly not enamoured of having a drunk aboard—closed the door and drove off!

Now what did she do? To her mind Gavin was fairly harmless, but the idea of dragging him up the stairs to the apartment and bedding him down on the sofa was one she did not wish to consider overlong. The problem was, taxis did not seem to pass by this area too often.

Erin had just decided on plan B, which was to open up the apartment, scrape Gavin off the wall he was clinging to and leave him sitting on the stairs while she went upstairs and phoned for a taxi, when to her surprise a taxi suddenly drove through the archway and into the courtyard!

What was even more surprising was that the man who stepped out, and asked the driver to wait, was none other than Joshua Salsbury! *Joshua Salsbury!* Erin did a double-take, her mouth falling wordlessly open.

She was still staring at him open-mouthed when, 'Need any help?' he drawled, flicking the briefest of glances in the direction of her sozzled escort.

This was no time to be swamped again by the utter humiliation of it. She looked from Josh to the man it seemed she had stood him up for. My stars—no contest! 'You wouldn't like to share your taxi with Gavin, I suppose?' she asked tentatively. 'I'd intended for him to go on in the taxi that brought me home, but the driver didn't wait.'

'I wonder why?' Josh muttered, but to her relief went first to have a word with his taxi driver and then to peel Gavin away from the wall. 'Come along, Gavin,' he said pleasantly. 'Time to go home.' Having been manoeuvred into the taxi, Gavin promptly settled down to quietly doze and clearly wanted no part in the proceedings. 'Where does he live?' Josh turned to ask Erin.

She gave the address Gavin had said, and designated this as the worst night of her life. She wanted nothing more than to go inside and shut the door on the world. Her thoughts were on going straight to bed, burying her head under the bedclothes and hoping this would all look better in the morning—some hope—when Josh Salsbury shut the door on the sleeping Gavin and went to talk again to the driver.

She saw money change hands, but was staring thunderstruck when Josh stood back and it suddenly dawned that the taxi was going to drive off—leaving her standing there, with him!

'T-taxis aren't too frequent around here,' she informed him witlessly.

Josh Salsbury turned and, staring down at her in the

security-lit area by her door, was silent for a moment or two. Then, very clearly, he said, 'Black, no sugar.'

She had never met anyone like him. But, getting herself together, she rather thought that by following her—and she had no idea why he had done that—and seeing Gavin on his way as he had, he was perhaps owed a cup of coffee.

'Come up,' she said, turning and unlocking her door. She felt very unsure of her ground here, and she enquired as he followed her up the stairs, 'Have you been here before?'

'Charlotte gave a small dinner party one evening,' he replied as they entered the sitting room.

In Erin's view it would have had to be a small dinner party. More than four people and it would be overcrowded. She could not help but wonder who his dinner partner had been. Probably one of the beauties whom Charlotte had once remarked were waiting for his phone call.

'Have a seat,' Erin invited, her voice calm, her insides a disaster. 'I'll just see to the coffee.'

She might have guessed he was not a man who was used to doing what he was told. He came and stood in the kitchenette doorway and watched while she deftly set the kettle to boil, got out cups and saucers and a jar of instant coffee.

'Er—why did you follow?' she asked. 'I mean, you didn't have business this way, did you?'

He shrugged. 'You didn't look as though you were enjoying being pawed.' As she had known, he had not missed Gavin clutching a too-intimate hand on her thigh. She hoped she wasn't looking as red as she felt. 'And my plans for the evening had been scuppered,' Josh added, his expression solemn as he fixed her with a steady grey-eyed gaze.

Oh, heck! She wanted to apologise, but felt hot all over at the thought of having to give him any sort of truthful explanation. 'How is your father?' she asked abruptly.

'He's mending,' Josh replied, her swift changing of the subject not lost on him, she knew.

'You went to see him this evening?' she queried, starting to feel a little desperate and wishing that the kettle would hurry up and boil.

He nodded. 'Your parents are well?' he enquired conversationally.

She wanted him to go. She was feeling uncomfortable. Parents plural meant a father and a mother. She did not want her mother anywhere near this conversation.

'Yes, thank you,' she answered primly, and with utmost relief saw that the kettle had boiled. She made coffee, loaded it on to a tray and calculated it would take five minutes, ten at the most, for him to drink his and then be on his way. Now, what the Dickens was she going to talk to him about for ten minutes that cut out family background?

Josh carried the tray into the sitting room and, as big as he was, seemed quite at home in the small room. She had opened her mouth to offer some polite piece of conversation about his work when he forestalled her by commenting, 'I assumed you were unmarried, and not "anything".' Batting back at her her own question, when he had asked her out, if he was married or 'anything'. 'Should I also assume that Gavin is your "anything"?'

'Grief, no!' she exclaimed before she had time to think. 'I—er…' To explain would be impossible. How could she explain anyway? She had given up dinner with the good-looking, non-pushy man opposite—for an evening in a hotel bar with Gavin! 'Is your coffee all right?' she asked jerkily.

'Perfect,' he replied, though she suspected he was not too well acquainted with instant coffee. 'You sound nervous?' he observed calmly.

'I'm not!' she hastened to assure him, hastily adding, 'It's just that this is a new experience for me—entertaining someone to coffee without my father there.' Oh, drat. Oh, confound it! She wanted to die. She saw Josh Salsbury still, as though arrested by what she had just said. She would have welcomed a faint.

'You've never...?'

'Forget I said that!'

'Until you moved here—what? Five weeks ago?' Almost six, actually. 'You'd lived in Gloucestershire with your parents?' Josh queried slowly.

Oh, families! She did not want to go in that direction. 'My parents are divorced. I lived with my father.'

'Who, by the sound of it, looked after you very well.'

'I'm twenty-two,' she told him, as if that had anything to do with it.

'I'm thirty-five—how do you do?' Josh responded—and she just had to laugh. She saw his glance go to her mouth, as if he liked to see her mouth curve upwards. But she was not happy with his questioning when suddenly, as if the thought had just come to him and had shaken him a little, he said, 'You're a very beautiful woman, Erin, but I'm getting a very distinct impression here that you are not altogether—worldly-wise.'

'I...' am, she wanted to say, but the lie stuck in her throat. 'I'd like to be!' she said, and *did* then go crimson. 'Oh!' she wailed. 'I wasn't hinting or anything!' Why didn't the floor open up and swallow her? Was she really having this conversation?

'You're not telling me you have never...' he paused, then resumed, 'had a boyfriend?'

'Of course I have!' she defended. 'Actually, I'm between boyfriends at the moment. Oh, heck, this is coming out all wrong!'

'What happened with the last boyfriend?' he asked evenly, charmingly, and so entirely matter-of-factly that it didn't seem at all startling to Erin.

Which was perhaps why she did not find it startling that she should honestly reply, 'I wouldn't. So Mark went to bed with a woman I'd thought was one of his *ex*-girlfriends.'

It did not take Josh but a second to sift through what she had said. 'Have you ever?' he asked, point-blank.

Been to bed with anyone? 'No, but I'm going to as soon as I can!' she replied openly—and stared at him, stunned. Had she really just said that? 'I only had one gin and tonic—my mouth seems to be running away with me.'

'It's a rather lovely mouth. Is that why you left home? Because you couldn't—mmm—indulge in extracurricular—activity—while under your father's roof?'

'You make me sound terrible.'

'Not at all. You're a healthy young woman with a young woman's natural—appetites. You're obviously finding your chaste state a touch irksome.'

'Everybody seems to be having a better time than me,' she found herself confiding.

'I'm sure they're not,' he replied kindly. Erin fell a little bit in love with him. 'Have you anyone in your sights?'

To make love with? 'I haven't met anyone yet,' she

replied, looking at one who might well be one such. 'I think I must be a little—er—fastidious!'

He could have been offended—she had, after all, in effect turned him down. A date with him anyway. But he wasn't offended. 'Is this the complication you spoke of?' he asked.

She shook her head. 'No,' she replied honestly.

Josh looked into her eyes for a second or two longer, then got to his feet. 'Don't be in too much of a hurry, Erin,' he advised quietly. 'It will be a special time for you. Choose carefully.'

'I'll come down with you and make sure the door is locked when you've gone,' was all she could think of to answer.

Then she wished she had left him to let himself out, because the problem was that there was hardly any room at the bottom of the stairs. Barely enough room for two people to stand together. They bumped into each other, and as she looked up uncertainly into Josh's eyes so he looked into her eyes for long moments. And then, unhurriedly, he took her into his arms, and gently he kissed her.

Her heart thundered as his kiss came to an end. He still had his arms loosely about her, and she stared up at him with stunned eyes. She transferred her glance to his wonderful mouth; she wanted to feel that exciting mouth over hers again.

She looked into his eyes again, and what he was reading in hers she did not know. But as he gathered her that little bit closer to him so his head came down again, and she was on the receiving end of the most sensational warm and lingering kiss. Her lips parted and his kiss deepened—and as her head spun she held on to him.

Their kiss ended, and as unhurriedly as he had taken

her in his arms Josh was releasing his hold and looking down into her slightly bemused face. 'It's time all good girls were in bed,' he stated calmly—when she was feeling a churned-up mass of she knew not what. 'Goodnight, Erin,' he bade her, and just like that he went—leaving Erin totally bewildered.

A state she was in for the week that followed. Again and again she recalled his fantastic kiss. And again and again she went through a whole range of emotions, wondering if—even though she had told Josh that she had not met anyone she wanted to make love with yet—he had thought from her response to him that she had changed her mind about that. Her face flamed because she quite honestly did not know how she would have reacted had he added 'but not alone' to his 'It's time all good girls were in bed.'

Another week went by, and gradually Erin started to adjust to what had happened. She began to be more comfortable within herself, and to not feel so flustered when each day she would recall different parts of her conversation with him. Never had she been so open with any man.

So what was so special about him? Well, just about everything, she supposed. He made all other men non-starters, at any rate.

Gavin Gardner didn't so much as figure, though he did offer his most abject apologies when they next bumped into each other. 'I well and truly blotted my copybook, didn't I?' he said, shame-faced.

'You were sloshed,' Erin replied.

'It was that deal,' he explained. 'They don't happen like that every day.' And, ever the trier, 'Are you going to let me make amends by coming out with me again?'

'There's only so much of a good time a girl can take,' Erin told him lightly.

She had half hoped that Josh Salsbury might give her a ring, even though nothing was changed and she would still be unable to go out with him. But she felt it would have made her feel better had he shown so much as a small spark of interest. But, all too plainly, whatever spark had ignited for him to invite her to have dinner with him that one time had died an instant death.

If her social life was nothing to rave over, however, work-wise everything was going splendidly. Her work for Charlotte was coming to an end, the catching up more or less completed, which left her with just the day-to-day matters to deal with. Erin had had a word with her and said that really she didn't now require her services, and Charlotte had agreed that if the right job came along she could leave in under the three months they had initially agreed on. But only if it was the right job and they absolutely needed her to start right away.

And the right job *had* come along.

Erin had seen one or two that looked interesting, but it was 'secretary with ability to adapt to changing situations' that had caught her eye. Though when she'd seen who the firm advertising was, none other then Salsbury Engineering Systems, she'd been a little hesitant. Josh and his father were at the head of that company—should she apply? It sounded a very busy office. She liked to be busy.

Erin had given the matter some long and in-depth thought. She wanted to stay in London. She wanted a job that kept her busy—no chance of boredom there. She'd read the advert again. It was in the experimental division, which was several miles away from the main offices. Very probably Joshua Salsbury never showed his face there.

She had applied, been interviewed and had liked what she saw. They had liked what they saw, too, and had been keen for her to start whenever she was available.

'I'm going to miss you!' Charlotte had lamented, when Erin had arrived back at Fisher Fabrics and said she had agreed to start her new job the following Monday. 'But you're still living at my place, so we won't lose touch. And of course you'll come to my wedding. But, oh, Erin, it's just not going to be the same without you here.'

As Erin had anticipated, she thoroughly enjoyed her work at Salsbury Engineering Systems. It was varied, often more dogsbody work than secretarial, but she did not mind a bit. She worked with a fair-sized group of super people, but in three weeks knew everyone by name and, importantly, knew what she was doing. She no longer had to ask questions, but was confident in what she was doing.

While a few of the men there were mature boffins, who treated her as they might a daughter, there was a younger element with whom she also got on with very well. In particular Stephen Dobbs, a man in his late twenties who had one day surfaced from his work and come to find her.

'If you're not busy tomorrow night, and otherwise unattached, we could go and have something to eat somewhere?' he had suggested.

Erin had looked at him, tall, fair, and bespectacled. She had wavered. She liked her own company. But, hey, she could spend time on her own back in Croom Babbington.

'That sounds very nice,' she had replied. He had beamed, and she had decided to enjoy herself.

Which she had. He was pleasant, and not pushy. They had kissed, briefly, on parting—there was no spark there.

She went out with him several times, and they kissed more warmly, but that spark just could not be conjured up, and she knew then that things between them were never going to go further than friendship. Which was what she told him on their next date. And he proved as pleasant and nice as she had thought. He accepted what she said, and asked her out again.

Erin had other offers to wine and dine too, and wouldn't have been human if she hadn't felt flattered at such attention. But she was not interested in dating more than one man at a time, even if her friendship—it could hardly be called a relationship—with Stephen was going nowhere. If her thoughts drifted too many times to Joshua Salsbury, though, then only she was going to know of it.

Life plodded on. She went home to Croom Babbington each weekend, either on a Friday or a Saturday, with nothing too earth-shattering happening. Then, on the Tuesday of her fourth week at Salsbury Engineering Systems, several things out of the ordinary occurred.

Firstly she received an invitation to the wedding of Charlotte and Robin. By then that sensation of love she had experienced for Josh Salsbury made Erin very much want to see him again. He would be at the wedding, she knew, and even if she didn't get to talk to him she would see him. The decision was made for her. The wedding was to be in Bristol. She would go.

The next thing that happened was that she was passing by the office manager's office when the door opened and

Ivan Kelly, the manager, came through. 'Ah, Erin! I was just coming to see you!' he exclaimed.

'What can I do for you?' she offered cheerfully.

'How's your shorthand for technical matter?'

'It's come on by leaps and bounds since I've worked here,' she replied with a smile. Clearly he wanted her assistance with something involving deeply technical matter.

'The Prof is holding a meeting this afternoon, and Kate's called in sick.'

The Prof, otherwise know as Professor Joseph Irving, had the sort of mind that went up corridors few others were likely to go. 'You want me to take the minutes?' she queried, it requiring little guesswork, her thoughts already on sitting up and taking notice.

'Would you?'

'I'd love to,' she obliged, hoping it would not be too complicated a meeting.

It was not. But Erin was kept alert, and only at the end of the meeting, when the Professor had finished and everyone had begun to tidy their notes, did she feel free to relax.

But then something happened that made her tense and her heart suddenly start to beat faster. For, contrary to her opinion when she had decided to apply for the job that Josh Salsbury probably never showed his face there, all at once the door opened and, tall, dark and as totally good-looking as she remembered, he came in. The head of the experimental department came in with him, but Erin barely noticed the other man.

She felt her cheeks burn, and was glad everyone was too taken up with the chief executive's unexpected arrival to be glancing her way. The last time she had seen him she had been in his arms! He had kissed her, lingeringly. It had been oh, so wonderful. She had never forgotten the feel of his mouth over hers.

She saw a very pleased Professor Joseph Irving shake hands with him, and watched as the Professor reacquainted Josh with some of the senior members of his team.

Sorely needing to get herself under control, Erin looked away. But she still felt all of a mish-mash inside when she looked back again. She was glad that her hot burn of colour had subsided, and when she noticed that some of the junior members had started to drift back to their workstations she realised that she had no business sitting there any longer.

Glad to have something to clutch on to, be it only her notepad, Erin got to her feet. The Professor was by that time well into deep and technical conversation with Joshua Salsbury, and Erin knew as she neared them that Josh would not even glance her way.

Wrong! He did glance at her, albeit that he did not appear to take his attention from what the Professor was saying. Grey eyes met violet eyes, and for all Josh Salsbury did not interrupt the Professor to say a word to her—she'd hardly expected him to; it was, after all, the Professor he was obviously there to see—Josh's glance moved briefly down to her mouth, as though he too was remembering her lips beneath his, and as though she was not the only one who had never forgotten their kiss.

As if! Impatient with herself, impatient with him, Erin went swiftly from the room. She stopped by her desk, but only to drop down her notepad before going swiftly on to shut herself away in the ladies' room. As if was right. For heaven's sake, get things in proportion. Joshua

Salsbury had probably kissed half a dozen women since then!

Well, it was for sure she didn't care—so why did she find seeing him again so totally upsetting?

CHAPTER THREE

NOTHING seemed, or was, the same after Josh Salsbury's visit. There was still a buzz about the place when Erin went into work the next day. When she learned the reason for that buzz, her emotions went haywire.

Apparently Josh seldom visited the experimental division, preferring to leave them alone to get on with what they did best. But a facility was now available within the head office of Salsbury House, and, while they would still hold the larger plant at their present site, a minor experimental section, including support staff, would be moving at short notice to Salsbury House.

'Do *we* have to go?' Erin asked Ivan Kelly, her immediate boss. She felt vulnerable somehow, all sort of shaky inside, and didn't know that she would have applied for this job had she known she would be spending her working life under the same roof as Joshua Salsbury.

'Most definitely,' Ivan answered. 'The Prof's been badgering away for ages about the shortage of space here. He's over the moon that at last his voice has been heard. You don't mind, do you?' Ivan thought to ask. 'Does working over there represent some kind of transport problem?'

'No, not at all,' Erin answered, and smiled. 'I can just as easily get there as here.'

But do I want to? she had to question. It was a fact that just seeing Josh Salsbury made her feel all funny and peculiar inside. But she consoled herself that, having detoured past Salsbury House on her way back from

Croom Babbington one Sunday, it was a large enough place for her never to ever bump into him.

Besides which, Erin discovered as the move progressed, and only two weeks later she transferred to her new working abode, that new working abode turned out to be a converted building adjacent to the rear of the main building. It had its own entrance, and apart from a need for someone to occasionally hand-deliver various figures to the statistics department, or take a note to some other department, she did not in fact, as she had supposed, work in the same building as Josh Salsbury.

Which in turn made her feel most mixed up. Because while she had shied away from the thought of perhaps daily running the risk of bumping into him in some corridor, the fact that now presented itself—that she might never see him again—was, she reluctantly admitted, a little disconcerting. Without thinking about it too deeply, she was glad she had written and accepted the invitation to Charlotte's wedding. She would see him then, anyhow.

On Thursday evening, a couple of days later, Erin rang her mother. Nina was home, but sounded so unlike her usual ebullient mother that Erin grew concerned. 'What's wrong?' she asked.

'Nothing's wrong!' Nina Woodward replied smartly. Too smartly.

Erin was not taken in, and did a rapid think. She was going out with Stephen Dobbs tomorrow, and although she would quite happily cancel the arrangement, she doubted her mother would be free on a Friday evening. 'Have lunch with me tomorrow?' she invited. And, when Nina hesitated, 'Don't worry. I won't tell anyone I'm your daughter.'

'I should think not!' her mother replied, and sounded

more like her old self when she added, 'I'm much too young to have a daughter your age!' Erin knew for a fact that her mother was forty-one, but felt pleased when she agreed to lunch. 'I'm in town anyway. But it will have to be a quick lunch. Phillipe is doing my hair at two-fifteen—a marvellous man.'

Erin's concern for her parent, which had been mollified the evening before, reared up again when over lunch her mother seemed unusually quiet and thoughtful. 'Something *is* wrong,' Erin stated.

'Don't be silly,' Nina responded, and, adept at changing the subject, 'I was surprised to hear you're working for Tommy Salsbury's outfit. How are you getting on?'

'Fine,' Erin replied. 'We've transferred over to Salsbury House, but—' She broke off as a reason for the difference in her mother came to her. 'That's it, isn't it!' she exclaimed. 'You're worried about him?'

Nina Woodward gave a start. 'Worried—about who?'

'Tommy. Mr Salsbury,' Erin pressed. 'Have you heard? Has he had a relapse or something?'

'How would I know?' Her mother sounded so totally uncaring that Erin knew she had jumped to the wrong conclusion. 'The last I heard Tommy was tearing up the laps on some rubber-belted treadmill.'

Erin was much pleased to hear that. By the sound of it, Josh's father was doing well in his recovery. 'What, then?' she insisted.

'Oh, for goodness' sake! You're just like your father! He was as stubborn as blazes once he thought he was on to something.' Erin said nothing, but sat quietly and waited. 'Well, if you must know,' Nina began a touch shortly, 'I've—um—met someone.'

'When didn't you?' Erin replied calmly.

'This one's—different.'

'Different?' Nina did not answer. 'How different?'

Her mother gave her an exasperated look. 'Well, he's younger than me, for one thing. Though not by much,' she added quickly.

'And?'

Nina smiled. 'He makes me laugh. He rings me in the morning and makes me laugh. He rings me in the afternoon and...' Her voice fell away.

'And you're in love with him?' Erin suggested gently.

'Oh, I wouldn't go that far!' Nina said sharply, but then, the edge going off her voice, 'But Richard does have that little—something extra.' She looked at her watch. 'And now I must fly. We'll do this again. Lunch. Soon.' She gathered up her belongings, genteelly air-kissed her daughter, said, 'Bye, darling,' and, as elegant as ever, her hair looking immaculate, as if she had just come from the hairdresser instead of being on her way to the salon, she was gone.

Erin paid the bill and went back to her office, hoping that things went well for her mother and Richard. She did not want either of them to end up hurt, though with her mother's track record guessed that Richard was the more likely candidate. With luck, perhaps he would keep well away from the 'marriage' word.

Erin went out with Stephen on Friday evening, and on Saturday she drove to Croom Babbington. She spent a quiet time with her father and drove back to the mews apartment on Sunday evening. And by Monday she was on a more even keel about—well, Josh Salsbury in particular. It lasted until Tuesday, when Ivan Kelly, looking enormously pleased about something, came seeking her out.

She looked at him. The cat who'd swallowed the

cream had nothing on him. 'You got all six numbers in the Lotto?' she teased.

'Not quite as good, Erin, but certainly a feather in the cap of this department.' She was pleased for him. They were a clever bunch, the people she worked with, and deserved every accolade that came their way. She was not so pleased, though, when, clearly bursting to share his news with her, he grinned hugely and said, 'Apparently your praises have been sung in high places.' Erin stared at him, mystified. 'As of now, you've been seconded to work for none other than the chief executive!'

Her mouth fell open, and while there was a kind of roaring in her ears Erin stared at him. 'Ch-chief executive?' she stammered.

'Only Mr Joshua Salsbury himself!' Ivan replied proudly. And, while Erin just stared at him, wide-eyed, 'I'm going to be lost without you,' he went on. 'But it will only be for two weeks—nine days, actually, while Mr Salsbury's PA is on holiday.'

'Me?' Erin managed, if faintly. 'I'm to act as his PA for...' Her voice trailed away.

'Oh, it won't be just you,' Ivan informed her jovially. 'It seems that the PA called in to substitute for Isabel Hill is having a hard time coping with the volume of work. You're to assist her.'

Erin was undecided whether to run right then—out from the building and back to the sanctuary of the mews apartment. But excitement was stirring in her bones. Though she made herself appear outwardly calm, at least, when she questioned, 'You're saying that I'm to work in Mr Joshua Salsbury's office?'

'If not his office, then the office adjoining.' Ivan looked at his watch. 'As of now, Miss Tunnicliffe, you are the temporary assistant to the temporary PA to the next chairman of this company. Hurry, now,' he urged, but smiled as he added, 'But don't forget to come back.'

Erin finished the work she had been doing and tidied up a few loose ends with the first rush of excitement fading to be replaced by questions. Her? Why her? It was all very flattering, and someone somewhere must have mentioned to Personnel that she did her job well—but still, why her? Salsbury Engineering must employ dozens of other business-trained secretary dogsbody assistants with the ability to float into any section and tackle whatever came their way. So—why her?

An hour later she stepped into the main building, heading for the top floor where Josh Salsbury had his offices, and began to worry that he might know nothing of whom Personnel had selected to assist his temporary PA. Would he be annoyed that it was her?

Erin started to feel more churned up than ever when she so easily recalled that day when she had taken the minutes of a meeting and Josh had appeared. He hadn't exactly looked through her, she recalled, remembering his glance to her mouth, the lips he had once kissed. But neither had he acknowledged her either.

Erin reached the office she was looking for, having worked herself up to anticipating that in about two minutes from now she would be making her way back the way she had come, Josh Salsbury having politely—or not—told her thanks, but no thanks.

Which was when her pride kicked in. Who did he think he was? She rapped smartly on the door and went straight in. Josh Salsbury was there, and was alone. She saw at once she had chosen his office instead of the PA's office, but that was all to the good. If he was to send her on her way, she would prefer that no one else overheard.

'I've been seconded here to assist your relief PA, but I can go back again if my face doesn't fit!' she charged hostilely—her insides belonging to anyone but her.

Josh Salsbury, tall and as good-looking as ever, rose to his feet and, even though she was across the room, appeared to look down at her. He studied her for several moments. But when she was ready to do the quickest about-turn in history—if not get thrown out for her sauce—'You must know you have a most beautiful face—that fits perfectly,' he drawled, making her heart leap about for all he hadn't made it sound like a compliment. 'But heaven alone knows from where you grew that tremendous chip on your shoulder.'

Shame me, why don't you! 'I didn't know if you knew it would be me—if you—er—w-wanted me.' Swiftly, feeling herself going red, she corrected that. 'If you wanted me working in your office.'

'Now, why shouldn't I?'

You saw fit to ignore me the other day. She almost said it, but realised in time that that would make matters between them too personal. And she was here to work. 'Er—shall I get started, then?' she asked.

'Come and meet Angela Toon,' he answered.

It was then that Erin started to learn what working in a top-notch office was all about. It had taken her a couple of days to get into the swing of things, but by Friday she could fully see and understand why Angela Toon needed someone to help her with the workload; and could only admire from afar the unknown PA, Isabel Hill, who was at present taking what Erin knew without a doubt was a well-earned holiday.

But by Friday Erin knew too, without a single, solitary question of doubt, that—she had fallen in love with Joshua Salsbury.

She tried to tell herself that it was ridiculous, that she hardly knew the man. But, while it might be ridiculous, it was also fact. She woke up thinking about him, went to bed thinking about him, and if that was not enough her dreams were filled with him.

She would have liked to believe that what she felt for him was nothing more than a passing infatuation, pure and simple. After all, there was much to admire about the man. While he could be tough if the occasion demanded it, and she had heard him, at others he was positively charming. The fact that he seemed to gobble up work like none other—the charge of nepotism could never be laid at his door—amazed her. He kept both her and Angela fully occupied. But, as well as loving him, Erin loved the work.

The days flew by. In stark contrast the evenings dragged by oh, so slowly. Even so, Erin turned down a dinner invitation from Stephen Dobbs when he rang—somehow she wanted only her own company.

Erin left work on Friday, telling herself that this was crass. She would never get Josh Salsbury out of her head this way. She resolved that the next time Stephen rang she would say yes. She might even ring him. She didn't.

She went home to Croom Babbington on Saturday, counted almost every tick of the clock, and returned to London on Sunday, eager and hardly able to wait to get to work tomorrow.

Angela Toon started with a cold on Monday, and, try though she did, she had a hard time keeping up. By Tuesday her cold was ready to break out, but by Wednesday it had arrived in full force.

Josh Salsbury came into the office after her fourth sneeze in quick succession, took one look at her runny eyes and red nose, and strode over to the coat rack and selected the coat that was hers. 'Much though we value your input, Angela, I'm afraid we're going to have to manage without you,' he informed her kindly.

'I'll be fine!' Angela protested thickly.

'After a few days' rest,' he assured her, helped her into her coat and told her not to think of returning before Monday. And, once she was gone, 'Ring Personnel,' he instructed Erin. 'You'll need an assistant.'

'Suddenly I'm promoted!'

'Less of the sauce,' he growled, and halted for a moment when Erin's lovely face lit up with laughter, then went back to his own office.

Was it any wonder that she loved him? Erin gave her attention to her work and put her hand on the telephone, ready to ring Personnel. But, recalling how it had taken her time to get the hang of the office, she changed her mind and went through to the next-door office instead.

Josh was already busy with something, but after a second or two he looked up, and Erin plunged straight in, 'I was thinking, Mr Salsbury—' She broke off, fascinated when he raised an eyebrow at her formal use of his name. So, okay, yes, they had kissed. 'Well, the thing is,' she rushed on, 'I can't see anyone Personnel find arriving here before lunch. That leaves only two and a half days to go before your permanent PA comes back.'

'Your point?'

Trust him to want to get straight to the point—it was his way; she knew that by now. 'The point is that it will take someone new a couple of days to get the hang of things up here—and by the time I've finished explaining everything I could have done whatever it is myself.'

'You're saying you don't want an assistant?'

'Well, I know I can't hope to be up to Isabel's standard. But, yes, that's what I'm saying.'

'You think you'll be able to cope on your own?'

She wanted to say a firm and confident Of course, but did not want him to think she was big-headed. 'Given I shall probably have to work late a couple of times. Yes,' she answered.

His glance slid to her gently curving mouth. Though she doubted he was recalling how their lips had met, or that he even remembered it. Then he flicked his glance back up to her lovely violet eyes. 'Go to it—Miss Tunnicliffe,' said he, who had only ever addressed her as Erin. 'Go to it.'

She laughed, and went back to her own office. She knew her work was going to seem awfully dull after she departed his office come Friday afternoon. She had thought she loved her work in Experimental, but now rather thought seeing the busy cut and thrust of business from up here had spoilt her.

Josh went out at midday and did not return until three, when she went in to see him with some queries. 'Still coping?' he asked.

'Having a lovely time,' she answered, and smiled.

His gaze stayed on her. 'I suppose you must be. Weren't you only going to be in London for a short while?'

It was the first time while working in his office that he had referred to the fact they had known each other outside of the office. 'I came, liked what I saw—' she smiled '—and decided to stay awhile.'

'Away from your father's parental protection!' Josh commented, and Erin felt all churned-up inside suddenly.

'I—er…'

'I've embarrassed you?'

You care? 'I go and stay with him every weekend.

Talking of fathers,' she said in a rush, 'how is your father?' And, having rushed in without thinking, felt obliged to go on, 'It must have been something of a shock when he had a heart attack.'

'He's doing well, and should, if he heeds medical advice, make a good recovery.'

'Oh, I'm so glad!' Erin said fervently, and caught Joshua-never-miss-a-thing-Salsbury's sharp look.

'You know my father?' he demanded abruptly.

'No, no,' she denied, and, fearful that she might give something away, placed the folder in her hands on his desk and spoke of work.

Back at her desk, she half wished she had used what she now saw as a tailor-made opportunity to tell Josh that, while she herself did not know his father, her mother had known him. Erin admitted that she wanted to tell him; it just did not feel right to *not* tell him.

But she had not missed that tough strand of protectiveness in his abrupt tone when he'd asked 'You know my father?', and on reflection she thought it better that she had stayed silent. She would have to put up with that feeling of guilt that niggled away at her, she realised. Because it seemed pretty plain to her that Josh was aware that Nina Woodward had had a hand in stressing his father into heart attack country. Josh would just love it, wouldn't he, if he knew that that woman's daughter was working in his own office?

She would just have to put up with feeling guilty. How could she tell him? She hadn't asked to work for him, but had loved every minute of it. And to tell him would, she knew without doubt, see her back in Experimental quicker than that. Worse, Josh would probably refuse to countenance her working anywhere at all in Salsbury Engineering Systems. She'd be thrown out, her feet never touching the ground. No, she couldn't tell him. Quite definitely, she could not. While she was working for the company she might chance to occasionally see him, remote though the chance was. And, who knew? He might want cover again one day, should his PA be away again, and Personnel might call on her services once more.

Erin sighed. She loved him. Weak, feeble she might be, but she did not want to close the door on the chance to see him again—however remote that possibility might be.

But Erin did not like what falling in love had done to her. She did not enjoy the thought that she was being weak and feeble. So she determinedly ousted Josh Salsbury from her thoughts and got on with what she was good at: her job.

Even so, even having put in a good day's work, she still had to work late that night. She did not mind a bit. Josh had left his office around four on some business or other. He had not returned by the time she was ready to leave.

She tidied her desk, realising that she must guard against him seeing anything of her feelings for him. Going smartly from the building, she recalled how easily he could make her laugh, and Erin resolved then that there was no way he was ever going to know what he had done to her.

'What time did you work until last night?' he asked when she went in the next morning.

'Did you want me for something when you got back?' she asked in reply.

He shook his head. 'I was just impressed by the amount of work you cleared while I was out.'

He must be referring to the typing she had locked

away in his drawer prior to going home. 'Some have genius thrust upon them,' she cheerfully misquoted—and loved it when *he* laughed.

The day went well. They worked hard and in splendid harmony together. Erin feared Experimental was going to be only half as stimulating after this.

'Have you much more to do?' he asked, coming into her office some time shortly after six.

'Not so much,' she answered. And, noting that he appeared to be about to leave, 'Just off?'

'I've a dinner engagement. I'd prefer not to be late.'

Ferocious green spears of cruel jealousy slammed into her. He was going home to shower and change and get ready to call for some luscious lovely! Momentarily Erin felt she hated him. But it was an emotion of the moment and then she was swiftly recalling how she had resolved that there was no way he was going to see how it was with her. So, even while she was feeling totally devastated—ridiculous, she owned, but who said love was reasonable?—she looked down to tidy the papers in front of her.

'Either you've got it or you haven't,' she trotted out with a flick of a glance up at him.

He held her glance, making her unable to look away. 'True,' he agreed, and added, 'And you're a lippy little trollop.'

And she had to laugh. In spite of herself she had to laugh. 'Lippy, maybe. But trollop? I'm working on that.'

'Still?' He seemed interested that she had not yet carried out her stated intention to 'whatever' as soon as she could.

'I'll get there,' she assured him. And, feeling all hot and bothered inside at this personal turn, she looked from him, picked up her pen and, without the least idea of what she had been doing, said, 'Goodnight,' and leafed unseeingly through a few sheets of typewritten matter.

'Goodnight, Erin,' he answered quietly. She did not look up again until she heard the door close behind him.

She did not sleep at all well that night. For one thing what fractured sleep she did find was interspersed with dreams of Josh Salsbury dancing the night away with some sylph in his arms.

Erin journeyed to work on Friday with her stomach all knotted up, because this was her last day of working with him. Isabel Hill would be back in harness come Monday, and that would be that.

Erin had just crossed the road to Salsbury House when, to set her heart fluttering, Josh Salsbury stepped up to the building with her. 'Where did you park your car?' he enquired in friendly fashion as, reaching the door, he opened it and waited for her to precede him.

'I don't use my car for work. It's easier to use public transport to get here,' she replied, and as they walked over to the lifts she fought to get herself together, green barbs doing their nasty work again—he was always, but *always* in first! Always early! All too obviously he'd had one very late night!

Others joined them in the lift, which gave Erin a chance to get herself in more of one piece. But the lift emptied before it reached the top floor and she was very conscious of Josh standing next to her. 'Good meal?' she heard herself say, when she was sure she was not the tiniest bit interested. He didn't look as though he'd spent the whole night on the tiles, but what did she know?

'Not bad,' he replied. 'Went on a bit, as these things are prone to do.'

He sounded bored! Good! Erin hoped she had bored

him senseless, whoever she was. 'The meal?' Shut up, Erin. Shut up, do. You just don't need to hear any more.

'The evening,' he replied, to gladden her heart. 'You know what these business dinners are like.'

She didn't, actually, but as they entered their offices she could not deny that she was suddenly on cloud nine. He hadn't been wining and dining some lovely! Erin only just managed to prevent herself from breaking into a few choruses of 'Oh, what a beautiful morning'.

Matters took a downturn around ten-forty-five when, with the door between the two offices open, her phone rang and a male voice she had forgotten she knew said, 'Hello, is that Erin?'

'Speaking.'

'Mark Prentice,' he announced himself.

Mark Prentice? Mark Prentice? Click. Grief—and she had at one time thought him her boyfriend! 'Hello, Mark,' she replied, perhaps more warmly than she'd meant—probably because it didn't hurt a bit. If anything, he had done her a favour. But for him and that episode she might still be working for him in a nothing kind of job, might still be living in dear but—let's face it—dull as ditchwater Croom Babbington. 'How are you?' she followed up brightly, glancing through to the other office to see that Josh had looked up from what he was doing, as though suspecting the call might be for him. She placed her hand over the mouthpiece and told her employer, 'It's for me—personal,' and gave her attention back to Mark.

Apparently he was in London for the day and would like to take her to lunch. 'I know it's short notice, but you weren't answering your mobile yesterday and I didn't manage to get your office number until last night.'

From her father, obviously, who—equally obviously—would have insisted on knowing why he wanted it.

Erin kept her mobile switched off in the office, and realised she had not switched it on when she got home. But—lunch? In truth she didn't have time to take a full hour for lunch. Against that though, she didn't want Mark Prentice forming an impression that she had been so enamoured of him that she was still too hurt to see him.

'I'd love to have lunch with you,' she assured him brightly, made the arrangements, and put down the phone.

She went into the other office a few minutes later, but before she could carry out her intention to check a detail on the work she was engaged on her employer bluntly questioned, 'You have a lunch date?'

Had he asked nicely she might have replied in the vein that she didn't know how to contact her lunchee, but that if Josh had something urgent he wanted doing she would contact the restaurant and leave a message for Mark. But Josh had not asked nicely. In actual fact his tone had been quite antagonistic. And if he was anti because she had taken a personal call in his time, then, after the way she had slaved for him, not to mention the extra hours she had put in, could *he* go and take a running jump!

So, instead of being the good little temporary PA, Erin fired straight back, 'Why should you have all the fun!'

A grunt was her answer. She went back to her desk. She would sort out her query when he was in a better humour. Honestly! He might be the big noise around here but, having come to realise that she was neither her mother nor her father but a person in her own right, Erin knew she did not have to put up with such treatment. Nor did she intend to!

Her annoyance with Josh Salsbury did not last long. In fact, loving him as she did, it amazed her that she could be angry with him at all. Love was making a non-sense of her, and she almost went and asked him if there was something in particular that he required actioning in the lunch-hour.

She did not do anything of the sort. Pride, another part of unrequited love, roused its stiff back and decreed she made herself a doormat for no man. If he felt he could speak to her like that, then he could suffer the consequences.

On the stroke of one she picked up her bag and left the office. A pity his door was by then closed—he wouldn't even notice!

Mark was waiting for her and kissed her cheek in greeting. He might have kissed her mouth, but she turned her head when her radar antennae went into action.

'You're as lovely as ever,' he said, holding on to both her hands.

How trite when he said it—how spine-melting it would have been had Josh Salsbury said it. 'You're look-ing well,' she replied, retrieving her hands.

They made their way to their reserved table and Erin sat opposite Mark Prentice and wondered—What on earth did I see in this man? She tried to be fair—he had seemed quite something back in Croom Babbington. But she had left Croom Babbington three months ago. And she had since met many different men, men at work, Stephen Dobbs. Nice men all. Even Gavin Gardner. So perhaps she had grown a little since leaving her home village. True, she had also met Joshua Salsbury who, without even knowing it, made all other men fade into the background. But, whatever had happened to her since she had left her home, Erin knew that were Mark Prentice to ask her on a date tonight—and it had little to do with the fact that he had taken his 'pleasures' elsewhere—she would not have accepted.

Which was a pity, because that was more or less what he did ask, barely into their starters. 'I've missed you, Erin,' he said soulfully across the table.

Perhaps she should have felt guilty that *she* hadn't missed *him*, not in the slightest. 'I'm sure your new secretary is very good at her job.' She chose to tactfully misunderstand him.

'I wasn't talking about work.'

So much for tact! She didn't believe he'd missed her anyway. It had taken him three months to find out he'd missed her! 'How *is* work? I expect business is as good as ever?'

'I was wrong to do what I did,' he pressed on, and Erin began to wish that she had never agreed to lunch with him.

'Well, it can't be helped now,' she answered lightly, and was a little shaken when he leaned across the table and caught a hold of her left hand.

'I was a fool, Erin. If only I could turn back the clock,' he said earnestly.

She quickly pulled her hand out of his grip. 'We all do things we—er—regret a little,' she said brightly, but felt dreadfully embarrassed.

'I regret what I did so much—so very, very much!' Mark declared ardently.

Oh, crumbs. 'You've no need to apologise,' was the best she could come up with.

'You mean you've forgiven me? You'll let us start all over again? You'll—'

'That's not what I'm saying at all,' Erin butted in quickly. And, with more tact than he deserved, 'It just isn't on, Mark. I live and work here now. We'd never see each other.'

'You come home every weekend,' he came back speedily, encouraged rather than discouraged, as she'd intended. 'Your father said you did when he told me to call around and see you when you came home tomorrow if it was so urgent.'

She stopped him right there. 'I'm sorry, Mark.' There was no way to dress it up. 'I don't think our getting back together is a very good idea.'

He took some convincing, but at last he appeared to accept that he didn't stand a chance. The restaurant was crowded, the service slow and, too late realising that to meet Mark at all had been a mistake, all Erin wanted to do was to get back to the office with all speed. The lunchtime seemed to go on for ever.

'Perhaps we'll bump into each other at the weekend?' Mark suggested hopefully as they parted.

'We may well do,' she said smilingly, and suffered another kiss to her cheek, knowing she was going to take jolly good care not to 'bump' into him.

She was late getting back to the office. The dividing door now stood open and she was in full receipt of Josh Salsbury's baleful glare when she went in. But when she knew she would work late to make up for any time lost—perhaps because she owed him the courtesy, or perhaps because she couldn't bear to be bad friends with him, or maybe a mixture of both—she went through to apologise.

'Sorry to be late back,' she trotted out prettily. 'The waiters were rushed off their feet. You know how it is.'

What she was expecting she had no idea, probably

some kind of, Now you're here, shall we get on? So she was more than a little taken aback when, tersely, he questioned, 'Mark's the one you left home over?'

Startled, Erin stared at her employer, more surprised that he had remembered her telling him about Mark than anything. 'I—er—don't actually recollect Mark having too much to do with my decision,' she replied, while trying to recall if he had figured in her decision at all.

'He's the one who bedded an ex-girlfriend when you declined the offer,' Josh documented. And, while Erin was still staring at him, but unable to deny it, 'You're surely not thinking of going back to him?' he bit shortly.

What was this? She'd only come in to apologise! 'That's another offer I declined,' she answered stiffly, and was halfway to the door when Josh's voice stopped her.

'He wants you back?' Erin was not happy with this conversation. It didn't seem quite right, somehow, to be discussing someone else's emotions. But Josh had his answer anyway. 'You dumped him,' he detailed. 'In effect, you dumped him.'

She opened her mouth to say it was none of his business, but then to her horror heard herself say something she had never, ever thought that she would say. 'I felt obliged to let him go,' she answered shortly, and went swiftly back to her desk, having to accept that while for sure she was her own person, there was without question something of her mother in her too somewhere!

Erin crashed into her work and put in a good hour on some complicated material, her mood lightening because when she went in to see Josh with a query he had lost his short edge with her.

It did not last. They had a lot to get through, and he was a work-oriented man, and did not care for interruption when the phone rang and it was another personal call for her.

'Oh, hello, Stephen,' she answered with a smile when she recognised his voice.

'Are you doing anything tonight?' he asked, and followed up with, 'How's your bowling arm?'

She laughed. 'I don't have one.' And as for going out that night, the pace they were going she'd be ready to flop at the end of her working day—always supposing she finished work before midnight. 'Tonight's a bit difficult,' she said, and, aware just then of Josh's impatient movement when he must have realised she was dallying in his time, 'I'll see you on Monday.' She closed the call, knowing that she'd be returning to Experimental come Monday.

'See you then,' he accepted happily enough, and they said goodbye.

It was not a figment of her imagination that J. Salsbury Esquire had gone crotchety again. 'It sounds as if you've moved on!' he snarled the moment she'd put down the phone.

'You know how it is, I'm sure,' she coldly bit back.

They worked in stony silence, managing, just, to be civil when business decreed they talk to each other. They worked without a break. She supposed she could have gone and got him a cup of tea, but she was feeling stubborn.

What a way to end what had started out as a fantastic nine days, she mourned when, gone seven that evening, she finished the last of her tasks.

She prepared her desk, ready for Isabel Hill to take over on Monday, left appropriate notes in Isabel's desk drawer regarding pending matters, and went in to say goodnight to the man she still loved—even if he was being a pig of the first water. Erin felt certain then that she would never again be called on to work for him. And since the only time she had ever bumped into him was that morning—using an entrance that she would not use when working in Experimental—she knew that, apart from Charlotte's wedding, she was unlikely to see him again.

He looked up just as Erin opened her mouth to tell him she was off home. 'You look tired!' he grunted.

'What every girl just aches to hear!' some snappy part of her she was not too familiar with erupted.

He gave her an icy look, then glanced at his watch, saw they had been hard at it for the past five hours and capped his pen. 'I'd better take you for something to eat,' he declared.

Don't force yourself, she fumed as he rose to his feet. 'I had a big meal at lunchtime, thanks all the same!' she retorted, her stubborn hat well and truly in place as she denied herself the chance to sit at a table with him.

Nothing more to be said, she went quickly back into the other office, picked up her bag and smartly got out of there. Thank you so much for all the hard work you've put in! Erin fumed. I so appreciate it! Eat with him? She'd sooner *starve!*

She calmed down a little as she walked along. She was heading in the direction of the tube station when she suddenly became aware of a long sleek dark car purring beside her. She stopped. The passenger door opened.

'Get in!' Josh Salsbury commanded. It was not a request, but an order.

About to tell him to get lost, Erin hesitated, and *she* was lost. She got in. The car picked up speed, and when he headed in the direction of the mews apartment she knew that he had accepted that she did not want anything to eat but that he was making it his business to see that she arrived home safely.

They drove in silence, but she didn't mind. He had said she looked tired. Tired was how she felt, and, given that she had been stubborn about not eating with him, she was glad she had given in about taking a lift home.

Though he must be tired too. Her heart started to warm towards him. The work he got through was phenomenal. He'd be glad to get home too.

Suddenly—belatedly, she admitted—she realised that he must be starving. He had been at his desk when she'd gone to lunch, and still there when she'd got back. Had he eaten anything at all?

By the time he drew his car to a stop at the mews apartment Erin was feeling mortified that she hadn't so much as fetched him a cup of tea. It made no difference that he was quite capable of fetching his own tea. She loved him; she should have looked out for him.

Impulsively she turned in her seat to look at him. 'I'll feed you if you like,' she blurted out, apropos of absolutely nothing. But, immediately recalling the last time he'd been in the apartment, she felt herself going a touch pink. And, at pains to let him know that this was no come-on, she rapidly followed up with a gulped, 'But I don't want any of that kissing business!'

He turned his head to stare hostilely at her. Oh, my word—kissing? He gave her a *killing* look. 'I'm hungry for neither!' he informed her curtly. And, if that wasn't enough to put her in her place, 'Some men might want to bed you, Erin Tunnicliffe—I'm not one of them.'

Open-mouthed, she stared at him. Then fury with him rocketed in. If he had anything more to say in the same acid vein, then she was not waiting around to hear it. She shot out of the car, jet propelled. The swine! The utter, unspeakable pig! In her view she had heard more than enough!

CHAPTER FOUR

As Erin had supposed, work in the upper echelons of Salsbury Engineering Systems had rather spoiled her for the experimental division. She missed the buzz, the excitement. She gave serious thought to leaving. But couldn't do it.

Two weeks went by and she gradually adjusted to being back in her own section. But her thoughts that she would never again be called upon to work directly for Josh Salsbury seemed to be underlined when, half anticipating that Isabel Hill might ask her up to the top floor to help sort out some query left behind, Isabel did not ring. She had sent her a note of thanks for managing so well in her absence—a note that included the information that a bonus would be paid into her bank at the end of the month.

Erin started to sleep badly. Josh was constantly in her head and she tried to get angry with him that when he could have just as easily written a 'thank you for managing' note he had not.

Which, she owned, wasn't quite fair to him. She'd seen the work he got through. Was he supposed to take time out of his busy day to write her a note? Get real. That was what PA's were for.

And why would he write her a note anyway? And if he did, which he wouldn't, would she read it and feel happy? She remembered the way they had parted and her pride reared up again. 'Some men might want to bed you, Erin Tunnicliffe—I'm not one of them'—as if she wouldn't tear any note he wrote into a dozen pieces!

Pride did not make it hurt any the less, though. He'd be lucky to get the chance! she fumed indignantly. Then she would recall his lingering kiss that time, and she knew his were the only kisses she ever wanted.

She was glad of her uncomplicated friendship with Stephen Dobbs. They went bowling together, and she met a few of his friends, and occasionally they went out in a small group—and she never once caught so much as a glimpse of Joshua Salsbury.

The logical part of her head demanded that she cut Josh totally out of her life. That she leave her job and remove even the remote possibilities of bumping into him. That would, of course, include writing a 'Sorry I can't come to your wedding after all' kind of note to Charlotte. But Erin could not do it. Instead she found she was scouring the shops for something 'a bit special' to wear on the day.

She found it two days before she was to drive to Bristol for the wedding. It was a pale violet shade, more of a deep lavender, that brought out the violet shade of her eyes to perfection. It was a sleeveless sheath of a dress made of silk, but with a chiffon overdress that had long sleeves. She felt she looked good in it

It was to be an afternoon wedding, and as she drove to Bristol on Saturday Erin was beset by a whole gamut of emotions because she would see Josh today. She had a tremendous need to know that she looked good.

Her confidence was given a boost in that when she reached the church several of the ushers made a beeline to direct her to her seat. She was escorted down the aisle by two men who introduced themselves as Greg Williams and Archie Nevitt.

She spotted Josh seated at the front, to the side of Robin, and her heart flipped over. Josh had his back to her but, to do her heart good, both Greg and Archie had decided to stay awhile and chat when Josh glanced back and across.

Their eyes met but, outwardly cool, even if her insides were all of a tremble, Erin looked from him and smiled up at Greg, in answer to something to do with him becoming better acquainted when his duties were over. Josh Salsbury might not 'fancy' her, but it was a salve to her pride that he should witness two men who clearly did.

'That makes two of us.' Archie was quick to stake his own claim. She smiled at him too.

But, their usher duties calling them away, Erin settled in her seat and studied the Order of Service she had been handed. When she thought she had herself under control she casually, pleasantly, glanced around, taking in with the sweep of her glance the man at the front to the right of the aisle.

Josh was no longer looking her way, had only glanced over for the briefest of moments anyway, and was now facing the front. Which gave Erin all the time in the world to feast her eyes on him. He looked particularly handsome in his morning suit. Looked both sharp and relaxed, sophisticated yet friendly. She loved the way his hair, kept short, wanted to bend into the back of his neck.

She wished things had been different. Wished she could have told him about her mother. But, then again, how could she? The last time she had seen him he had accused her of dumping Mark. More than ever now she could not tell him that her mother had known his father quite well, reveal that her mother was Nina Woodward, the woman who, a week before Thomas Salsbury had suffered a heart attack, had dumped him. No way did Erin want to see outrage in Josh's eyes as he noted, like dumping mother, like dumping daughter.

'Shall I sit with you?'

There were others in the pew, but not only did Greg Williams move into the pew to keep her company, Archie Nevitt squeezed in too. The fact that two of the ushers had for the moment completed their duties was a fair indication that the bride had arrived.

She had, and Charlotte looked absolutely gorgeous when, on her father's arm, with bridesmaids following, she came down the aisle in a cloud of white.

Erin felt quite emotional as Charlotte and Robin exchanged their vows, but during other parts of the service Erin's eyes would stray to Josh.

She had herself under control from then on, though. When the bride and bridegroom walked back up the aisle, followed in procession by their parents, and then the best man with the chief bridesmaid on his arm, Erin was intent on eye-to-eye contact with Greg Williams.

When she too walked from the church door she was still determined not to be caught with her eyes on the best man. That was not to say, however, that she wasn't aware of where he was most of the time.

And most of the time it seemed to her, as that green-eyed alien appeared again, to be paying more attention to the rather lovely chief bridesmaid than, in Erin's view, was strictly necessary. Erin gave her attention to Greg and Archie.

Because so many people had been invited the reception was being held at a hotel just outside Bristol, and not in the bride's home. Both Greg and Archie offered to drive her to the reception, but, their offers declined, they soon found her when in her own transport she arrived at the hotel.

Somehow or other, to the chagrin of Archie, Greg Williams managed to arrange it so that he sat next to her for the wedding meal. And, in truth, Erin was glad that he did. Greg was good-looking and attentive, and since she and Greg were seated facing the bridal table it was an aid to her pride that Josh Salsbury should not think her some unwanted wallflower.

Not that he appeared to have noticed that she was in the room, or was there at all, Erin considered, feeling inwardly an emotional mess as she outwardly smiled at Greg and kept up a pleasant line of banter with him. She'd like to know what Josh had just said to the bridesmaid that had sent her off into peals of laughter!

No, she wouldn't, Erin denied. She didn't care a bit. Which was why she laughed lightly when Greg said anything amusing, and why she kept her eyes mainly on him.

Speeches were made, toasts were drunk, people started to move around, mingle. Erin had a few words with Charlotte and Robin, and felt misty-eyed again when dancing began and the two executed the first waltz together. They looked a couple, a pair, a match, and she felt good inside that they had found each other.

Erin danced with both Greg and Archie, and with other men too, but saw no sign of Josh Salsbury wanting to dance with her.

Time started to drag, and when at eight o'clock Charlotte went to change out of her wedding dress Erin was wondering how much longer she could bear to stay. Josh was dancing with the bridesmaid—Erin had to admit they looked good together on the dance floor.

'I think I'll make tracks too,' Erin told Greg, who was

sticking close to her side when they later went outside to wave the bride and groom off to their secret honeymoon location.

'You can't go yet!' Greg protested. 'You haven't told me nearly enough about yourself. Besides...' he smiled down into her violet eyes '...we're getting on together so famously!' His smile became an arch look. 'Surely we should get to know each other—better still?'

Erin wasn't sure she felt too comfortable with that remark, but just then, as everyone started to wander back inside the hotel, she brushed heavily against someone. She looked up to automatically apologise, but as her heart started to pound so her voice dried in her throat.

'You're sure you know what you're getting into?' Josh Salsbury questioned coldly.

She heard him; no one else did. But she was more interested in showing him that she didn't give a light than in comprehending what he was talking about. 'Perfectly,' she answered loftily, and stuck her head in the air—and instead of going to her car, as she had intended, she turned to tell Greg, 'You're right, of course, Greg,' with small idea, until she caught his lecherous look of delight, what he was 'right' about.

They were on the dance floor, and he was holding her much too tightly, when it dawned on her that she had just agreed to get to know Greg Williams better. Couple that with Josh Salsbury's 'You're sure you know what you're getting into?' and warning bells started to ring in her head.

Those warning bells did not merely ring but started to clang out a tremendous clamour when the dance ended and Greg escorted her back to a table. He grabbed up a couple of glasses of champagne from a hovering waiter *en route*, and grinned as he said, 'Word has it that the hotel's full. But sit here while I go and sweet-talk the receptionist into finding us somewhere to lay our heads.'

She stared at him.

'I won't be long,' he promised confidently.

And while she was feeling too stunned by this turn of events to so much as squeak out a protest, Erin took a grip on the champagne glass in front of her. She knew then that, whatever erroneous signals Greg had been picking up, the time had come to tell him, and to tell him quickly, that wherever he was laying his head that night she wouldn't be there to share his pillow.

Agitatedly she played with the stem of the champagne glass, realising that some of the fault for those erroneous signals was well and truly hers—and Josh Salsbury's! It was only because Josh was there that she had been much more forward, flirtatious, even, than she would normally dream of being. It was only because she was trying to cover up what seeing him with 'the laughing bridesmaid' was doing to her, while at the same time hiding that she loved the over-confident, over-everything swine that...

'Bolstering up your courage, Erin?' A silky-toned voice she would rather not hear just then broke into her thoughts.

She looked up sharply. Just what she didn't need! Josh Salsbury, having seen what was going on before she had recognised Greg Williams's intent herself, had come to mock her. Her eyes followed Josh's glance to the table, where her long dainty fingers were still in contact with the stem of the champagne glass.

'For your information, I've limited myself to only one glass of champagne!' she snapped.

He ignored her reply, hellbent, it seemed, on following his own line of thought. 'And I quote—"No, but I'm going to as soon as I can."' And as she just sat and stared at him, recalling how she had once more or less told him she was going to go to bed with someone as soon as she could, he went on to challenge, 'Do I take it you're about to embark on your "soonest" endeavour?'

Stunned, it took her a second to let what he had just said sink in. But a moment after that fury rushed in, and she was absolutely outraged. Of all the nerve! Of all the… 'And the reason I've limited my champagne consumption,' she flew, too incensed all at once to stop and wonder why she was explaining anything at all to him, 'is because I have every intention of driving myself back to London—alone!'

She was angry with herself then too, that she was actually *explaining* anything! And in a rush of further fury with him, and with the whole male population—Greg Williams included, that he should toddle off without so much as a by-your-leave to go and find them a bed for the night—she stormed to her feet, sparks positively flying from her eyes that Josh Salsbury should think what he so obviously did think.

'And for your further information,' she charged, her violet eyes on fire, 'to go to bed with some man could not be further from my mind. And if you see Greg Williams you can jolly well tell him that from me. The only place I'm going,' she hurled, incensed, 'is home!'

And, having delivered that outraged tirade, she spun furiously about. And though Josh moved fast, it was not fast enough; she went crashing into a marble pillar that she had known was there but had been too enraged to give thought to. She saw stars—then nothing.

She slowly became aware of voices, hers and—she was having a conversation with someone. That was to say someone was talking to her, asking her questions and making her answer. She wished they would shut up—she wanted to go to sleep. Hang it all, she had been sleeping so badly, and now—now that she had the chance to get some rest, now that she was ready to get some sleep—somebody was badgering away at her.

'How many fingers am I holding up?'

She opened her eyes—light screamed in—she quickly closed them again. The light hurt her eyes. 'If I tell you three will you shut up and go away?' she answered.

'She'll do,' said the voice.

Then she had funny dreams of Josh being there. But then, he was always in her dreams, so what was new? 'How are you feeling now?' he asked.

'How do I look?'

'Enchanting,' he answered.

She sighed. It was a lovely dream. She wanted to tell him she loved him, but some strand of modesty, even in her dream, held her back. 'Do you like me?' she asked instead.

'Who could help but like you?' he replied.

'Suitably non-committal,' she mumbled, and sighed again. 'Goodnight, darling,' she said softly.

'Goodnight, sweetheart,' he said in the same quiet tone.

'Would you kiss me?' she requested. 'Just a gentle kiss, like before.' There was a bit of a pause. But then she felt his lips gently touch her brow. 'Thank you, Josh,' she whispered.

'You know it's me?'

She felt so tired, so dreadfully tired. 'Who else would I let into my dreams?' she answered sleepily. 'Goodnight,' she bade him again. And, her dream closing down, she went to sleep again.

Erin awoke and didn't quite know where she was. She

was in bed, but it wasn't her bed. She was in a strange room and, while it was otherwise dark, there was a small bedside lamp on somewhere. It was not to the left of the bed, where she had been sleeping, but on the other side of the bed where—Josh Salsbury, his face turned towards her, was sleeping.

She smiled. 'I'm still dreaming,' she said out loud. But at the sound of her voice the man beside her opened his eyes and, bare-chested, sat up. And as he looked over to her so the knowledge stampeded in to Erin—*that she was neither dreaming nor asleep!*

'What...?' she gasped, amazed, her eyes hypnotised by his all-male naked chest for moments before she gained her second wind. 'Wh-wh...? *Get out!*' she screamed. Then, urgently countermanding that, 'No! Don't!' she squeaked, having no idea how naked the rest of him might be. 'I didn't...?' she questioned hoarsely, as she fought for a memory that just wasn't there. 'Oh, my head!' she groaned, as the mother and father of all headaches made its presence felt.

She abruptly and tightly shut her eyes. And the next time she opened them it was to see that Josh had moved quickly to grab up a light robe from somewhere, had it about him and was coming round to her side of the bed. 'Here, take these,' he said quietly, handing her a couple of tablets and reaching to the bedside table for a glass of water. 'The doctor left them. He said you might need them when you woke up.'

Hearing Josh speak for the first time made it certain for Erin that this wasn't any dream. Josh was here, truly here! And he was real!

But various other matters were jostling for precedence in her head. Though first she sat up and swallowed down the painkillers. As Josh took the glass from her, and took a seat on the side of the bed, 'Doctor?' she asked.

'You knocked yourself out,' Josh enlightened her.

'At the risk of sounding like some B movie actress—where am I?' she asked.

'In a hotel just outside of Bristol.'

'Did I ask you to kiss me?' she found she was asking inconsequentially.

Josh grinned. 'You remember?' He seemed relieved. 'It wasn't such a difficult task.'

She made an effort to remember more. 'I've been to Charlotte's wedding, right?'

'Right,' he answered. 'You were encouraging Greg Williams to do his worst. Remember him?'

'Oh, grief, yes. You were accusing me of—um—trolloping,' she dragged from the painful reaches of her aching head.

Josh smiled at her description, but went on to explain, 'You had a crack at denting a marble pillar with your head—and came off second best.'

'I—fainted—um—knocked myself out, you said?'

'You went down like a sack of coal.'

'Thanks!' Very descriptive! But, growing more awake by the minute—not to mention aware—she began to feel a little panicky, and suddenly erupted, 'What the devil was I doing in bed with you?'

'Calm down, calm down!' He shushed her. 'There was a doctor in the wedding party. He needed somewhere to check you over, and since I had a room booked here, and I was the first one to you, I naturally offered my room.'

'That doesn't explain why we—we're sharing the same bed!' she inserted pithily.

'I knew you'd be grateful!' he retorted.

'What for?' she challenged suspiciously.

'You should be so lucky!' he rapped. 'I like my women responsive.'

'I bet you do!' she snorted. But did calm down a fraction to push forward. 'So, you had me brought to your room?'

'You were a dead weight.'

'You carried me?' she asked in surprise.

He shrugged. 'Somebody had to do it. Anyhow, you started to come round, and the doctor gave you the once-over and said you'd be okay, but to try to keep you awake for a few hours.'

'That was what all that talking was about in my dream?'

Josh nodded. 'Anyway, round about midnight the doctor looked in again and said you were fine, but that it might be an idea to see that you weren't left on your own for a while.'

'So you stayed?'

'There was nowhere else to go. The hotel's full and—come two o'clock—there are you, sleeping like a baby.'

'You watched me in my sleep?' she questioned, grateful—but embarrassed.

'It wasn't such a hardship. You're extraordinarily beautiful, Erin.'

Her heartbeats fluttered. She opened her mouth, but as it sank in that Josh thought her extraordinarily beautiful she couldn't think of a thing to say. 'Um—so...?' she murmured.

'So there are you, two in the morning, sleeping soundly and in no danger, and there am I, by then admitting that I wouldn't mind a bit of shut-eye myself. You were sleeping well over to one side. There was more than half a bed going to waste.'

'So, just like that—you got in?'

He glanced humorously at her. 'I disposed of most of my clothing first,' he commented dryly.

'It's a relief to know you've got something on under there!' she snapped hostilely.

'Be it only my socks,' he tormented.

But she did not think it funny. Especially as, with talk of disposing of clothes, she had just then alarmingly realised that she was wearing next to nothing herself! She looked down to where most of her lacy bra was on view, and hurriedly felt beneath the covers to discover, with relief, that the other item of clothing she was left with was her briefs.

'Who undressed me?' she asked faintly, trying desperately hard to recall a friendly female face amongst the gathering. 'Charlotte's mother?'

'There were many offers,' Josh replied nicely. But, to shake her to the core, 'I thought you'd prefer that I did it.'

'You did it!' she echoed croakily, blushing crimson. She didn't doubt that he was no stranger to undressing the female form, but—honestly! But having been rocked at the revelation that he must have unzipped her dress and seen her semi-naked, there awoke in Erin a need to shake him for his trouble. Now what…? Got it! 'We've shared a bed, you and I,' she stated, and in no uncertain terms went on to stress, 'Contrary to anything—er—improper I may have been considering when I came to London, I'm still a good girl,' she informed him. 'Which means, I'm afraid, Josh Salsbury, that you're going to have to marry me.' How she said it with a straight face she never knew, but his look of total startlement was all the reward that she needed. She burst out laughing. 'Relax, I didn't mean it,' she confessed. 'I just wanted to see the whites of your eyes.'

His face creased with laughter. 'Cheeky baggage! I think we can safely say you're not suffering from concussion. Now, lie down and go to sleep.'

Erin loved to see him laugh, but that wasn't why she stared at him. 'With you here?' she objected.

'It's four in the morning,' he informed her.

Meaning, she supposed, that she'd have to be the most heartless of creatures to turn him out of *his* room in a fully occupied hotel at four in the morning. She thought of how especially good he had been in carrying her here anyway. But when the alternative to borrowing his bed for a few hours more was for her to get up and drive back to London, with her head still throbbing away, she just didn't feel up to it.

'Goodnight—morning,' she said, and lay fragilely down.

Josh got up and bent over her—her heart picked up its beat. But whether she hoped or feared he might kiss her brow again, he did not, merely reached down and pulled the covers up over her shoulders.

She supposed that there were a couple of chairs in the room he could stretch out in. 'Will you be warm enough?' she asked softly. Perhaps there was an extra blanket in the wardrobe. There were sometimes in hotels, she knew.

'Oh, I should think so,' he answered quietly. But shook her rigid by—obviously at the other side of the bed now—switching off the bedside lamp—and getting into bed with her!

Instinctively, and with more speed than thought, she jerked upright, and was already halfway out of the bed when he stretched out a long arm and caught a grip of her wrist. 'Oh, my head!' she cried, the fact that Josh was holding her there inconsequential as her sore head let her know she was not yet up to charging around.

'You'll feel much better with your head on a pillow,' Josh coaxed soothingly. Erin stilled. Oh, help her, somebody—what was she supposed to do? To rest her head on a pillow sounded the best suggestion she'd heard in a long while. 'You won't try to come the—er—old soldier?'

'Old soldier?' He laughed softly in the darkness. 'That's one you pulled out of your grandmother's cupboard,' he commented, but said no more, and she knew that he was leaving it up to her to decide whether nor not she could trust him.

Gingerly she lay down, and he was right; her head did feel better resting on a nice soft pillow. 'What happened to the bridesmaid?' she asked as the thought all at once jumped into her head.

He didn't ask what she was talking about, but answered quietly in the darkness. 'You put the kibosh on any plans I might have been nurturing in that direction.'

'Good!' Erin said, because she was glad, so glad, and not a bit remorseful. 'Goodnight—er—morning again,' she added, and turned on her side, away from him.

Josh let go of her wrist and likewise turned his back on her. And, this being something she knew she could never tell her father about, or anyone else for that matter—who would believe she could trust Josh so?—Erin closed her eyes. Could she tell her mother? Erin pondered, half-asleep, half-awake.

She came a little more awake, feeling agitated when the impulse came over her to tell Josh who her mother was. Erin turned over to face his back. 'Josh,' she said.

'Go to sleep, Erin,' he said sternly.

Her eyes became accustomed to the darkness. She was able to make out shapes in the room. She looked at Josh. He had an arm on top of the covers and she felt an almost undeniable urge to touch his shoulder.

She wouldn't, of course. This was a pretty electric situation. She had as good as told Josh that time that she thought it was about time that she made love with someone. And she knew now that she did not want to make love with anyone else ever; she knew that the only man she wanted to make love with was him. What would she do if just by touching him it triggered off a chain reaction?

Get yourself together, do, Erin, she scolded. Chain reaction nothing. Josh was tired. The poor man was more interested in getting some sleep than in reacting to her. Idiot! He wasn't the slightest bit interested in her.

Eventually she fell asleep, and after some sound rest she gradually started to surface. She felt snug and warm, and as if everything was just as it should be. She snuggled delicately against the source of warmth, her limbs moving. Her left foot came up against something. She explored to find what it was with her foot. It was a leg!

'When you've quite finished kicking me!' Josh Salsbury commented humorously.

Erin's eyes opened wide. She was in bed with Josh. Strangely, though, the fact that she had slept with him did not alarm her, nor the fact that it was broad daylight and Josh was lying on his back and she had an arm across him, his bare chest warm against the skin of her arm. She pulled her arm back under the covers.

'What time is it?' she asked, somewhat dreamily, she rather supposed.

'Time that one of us got up.'

'You can have the bathroom first,' she offered nicely.

'Too kind. How's the head?'

He turned his head to look at her, and she found herself staring into his warm grey eyes. Oh, she loved him so. She lifted her head from her pillow a fraction, and back down again, beaming her delight. 'Clear as a bell,' she answered.

'No pain? No muzziness?'

'As good as new,' she promised. But while knowing that one of them would have to move soon, yet knowing that this situation would never arise again, she wanted to stay there with him for as long as she could. 'It was a lovely wedding, wasn't it?' she offered conversationally.

'Do you always wake up talkative—or do we have that bash on the head to thank for it?' he teased.

Oh, Josh, Josh, Josh. 'I wouldn't know,' Erin answered. 'I mean, this is the first time I've woken up with anyone there *for* me to talk to.'

'What a sad life you've led,' he mocked.

And she loved every facet of him. 'What does one usually do when one wakes up with a—a…' What the Dickens were they? '…a friend?' she asked, and loved it when he seemed amused by her.

He sat up, and, looking down at her, with her tousled blonde hair spread over her pillow, he appeared ready to depart their 'friendship' bed. 'It varies. Sometimes this,' he said, and bent over to touch his lips to hers. Abruptly he drew back. 'Sorry, I shouldn't have done that—but you did ask.'

Her heart was hammering. 'If I asked again, would you do it again?' she questioned, someone she did not recognise seeming to be in charge of her.

Josh looked down at her. He shook his head. 'Not a good idea, Erin,' he said, and suddenly she felt dreadful.

'I'm sorry,' she mumbled, and turned her head away, too embarrassed suddenly to be able to look him in the eye any longer.

'Oh, Erin,' he said gravely, and, stretching out a hand to the side of her face, he turned her to look at him. 'It isn't because—' He broke off, then began again. 'Erin, I don't think you fully appreciate the vulnerability of your situation.'

She did. She knew perfectly well what the situation was. From her point of view soon, within a very short space of time, they would be going their separate ways. He would go back to being the chief executive of the firm she worked for, and she might never ever see him again. She loved him; she wanted these few minutes to go on for ever. More, she wanted something—a kiss, maybe, perhaps the feel of his touch—to remember.

'I'm never going to get to—um—experiment,' she complained sniffily.

And Josh looked down at her and smiled, brushing her face with the back of his fingers. 'You're just asking for trouble, issuing open invitations like that,' he said softly, but to her delight didn't follow through what had seemed his intention, to get out of bed and take up her offer of the first shower.

And then all at once that new person she had only just met was in charge of her again, was urging her on—that new person who perhaps might never have been aroused from slumber had she not fallen in love with him. And suddenly she heard this new person tease, with a smile in her voice, 'One kiss wouldn't hurt, surely?'

Josh looked at her, seemed a touch gently amused. 'I need a shave,' he refused politely.

I don't care—I love you. She stretched up a hand and touched his shoulder, a thrill shooting through her on contact with his skin. She looked from his shoulder and into his eyes, and saw him glance down to her inviting lips. Then to her great joy, and just as if he could not stop himself, his head started to come down.

'This isn't very clever,' he murmured—but at last his mouth touched down on hers. Gently he kissed her—and she loved it. He raised his head. 'Satisfied?' he asked, humour about him.

She smiled up at him. She felt shy, yet at the same time a little forward. 'You're joking?' she laughed.

He smiled down at her. 'Well, that's all you're going to get,' he told her.

But she wasn't having that. She had tasted his lips, and besides, instinct was telling her that he would not mind too much to kiss her again. She sat up, moved in close to him. 'Just one more,' she suggested. 'Um—a proper kiss.'

He raised a quizzical eyebrow—she loved him more than ever. 'You mean—like the grown-ups do?'

Oh, help. He'd barely touched her and she felt on fire for him. 'Please,' the brazen female in charge of her requested, and, fearing that he might withdraw his offer, she moved yet closer to him, her bra-covered breasts coming into contact with his broad chest.

'Erin,' he murmured on a groan of sound. And the next moment he had taken her in his arms, and she was on the receiving end of a very grown-up kiss. And it was like none other she had ever known.

His lips tempted hers apart as he drew the very soul from her. She responded by clinging on to him, holding him tightly when his tongue tormented and played with her lips, making her tingle all over when the tips of their tongues met.

The Harlequin Reader Service® — Here's how it works:

Accepting your 2 free books and gift places you under no obligation to buy anything. You may keep the books and gift and return the shipping statement marked "cancel." If you do not cancel, about a month later we'll send you 6 additional books and bill you just $3.34 each in the U.S., or $3.80 each in Canada, plus 25¢ shipping & handling per book and applicable taxes if any.* That's the complete price and — compared to cover prices of $3.99 each in the U.S. and $4.50 each in Canada — it's quite a bargain! You may cancel at any time, but if you choose to continue, every month we'll send you 6 more books, which you may either purchase at the discount price or return to us and cancel your subscription.

*Terms and prices subject to change without notice. Sales tax applicable in N.Y. Canadian residents will be charged applicable provincial taxes and GST.

If offer card is missing write to: The Harlequin Reader Service, 3010 Walden Ave., P.O. Box 1867, Buffalo, NY 14240-1867

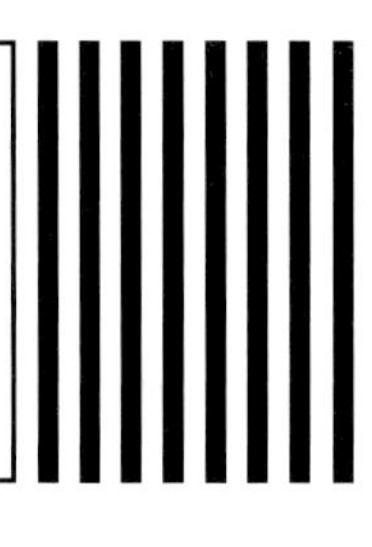

NO POSTAGE
NECESSARY
IF MAILED
IN THE
UNITED STATES

BUSINESS REPLY MAIL

FIRST-CLASS MAIL PERMIT NO. 717-003 BUFFALO, NY

POSTAGE WILL BE PAID BY ADDRESSEE

HARLEQUIN READER SERVICE
3010 WALDEN AVE
PO BOX 1867
BUFFALO NY 14240-9952

She pulled back when something akin to an electric shock shot through her. 'Josh.' She gasped his name.

'Shocked?' he queried, and she knew that she only had to agree that she was shocked and she would be sitting in the bed on her own.

For answer she smiled a mischievous smile. 'Delighted,' she gurgled, and, the time for requests gone—she no longer had to ask him to kiss her—she moved that small distance forwards and placed her lips against his.

It was an invitation for him to break down all her barriers, although in truth Erin didn't think she had erected any. She loved him so much it seemed only right and natural to be held and kissed by him.

She cared not that a few moments later Josh took charge of the kissing, their mouths meeting in such a prelude of passion that she felt dizzy from it. Nor was it only her lips that he pleasured. Erin felt his hands whispering over the silken skin of her back.

She knew yet more delight when he kissed her face and behind her ears, moving to kiss the arch of her throat. So enraptured was she by what he was entrancing her with that she almost told him of her love for him. But just as her lips parted he again claimed them, his mouth over hers while caressing fingers undid the fastening of her bra.

Erin started to grow a little shaky at this new ground she was on. But she feared that any objection she might make when he proceeded to remove her bra altogether would cause him to stop. And she did not want him to stop. She had been bereft in her love for him—she wanted solace. If there was a shyness barrier to get through she would get through it.

She held up her arms, the closer to get to him, and

felt the heat of his chest sear against her naked breasts. 'Oh, Josh!' broke from her before she could stop it.

'You're all right?' he queried, his eyes holding hers.

'Oh, yes, yes,' she told him hurriedly, dreadfully afraid he would take a non-reply as a negative answer and would make her bereft again by letting her out of his hold.

He smiled, and kissed her again, causing her breathing to temporarily halt when he pulled back and away from her—just as if nothing would do but that he must savour and see her breasts. 'You're exquisite,' he breathed, his eyes caressing the silken globes with their hardened pink tips.

But she was not feeling so very brave—or brazen—just then, so she moved in close to him, so to hide her breasts from his view. But he seemed to understand, and gently he kissed her. The next time his caressing hands came to the front of her she had herself under control, given that she swallowed hard when his warm sensitive fingers teased at those firm pink tips, and he moulded her breasts in his palms. 'Oh, Josh,' she cried involuntarily.

'Want me to stop?' he asked, sounding as if she only had to say the word and he would.

'Don't you dare!' she protested with a shy laugh, and loved it when he briefly laughed too.

Then he was tracing kisses over her nakedness, his lips finally reaching her breasts. He kissed first one and then the other, creating great swathes of wanting within her when he took the hardened pink peak of her right breast in her mouth, and tenderly toyed with the hardened tip of her left breast.

Josh's mouth took more of her breast as gently he moved her until they were both lying down. Transferring his mouth to her lips, he moved and came to cover her body with his, her briefs and his shorts the only covering between them—and Erin was in a frenzy of wanting.

'J-Josh,' she murmured shakily, but owned to a slight feeling of apprehension to feel his male hardness against her. That apprehension mingled with her by then quite desperate need of him as, their legs somehow entwined, she found she had effortlessly made room for him, and he appeared to as effortlessly have come to be captured between the silken unknown territory of her thighs. 'Josh,' she cried, and hated that hint of panic to be heard in the sound.

Especially did she hate it when Josh suddenly stilled, as though he had heard her panic too, and stopped dead. She knew it was so when, with a swiftness she found totally bewildering, he broke away from her.

'What?' she asked, wanting him back where he had been. 'I'm sorry,' she quickly apologised, it rapidly dawning on her that he thought her moment of panic meant no. 'I didn't mean…'

'You're not sure,' he cut in gruffly, going on, 'You need to be very sure, Erin.'

'I am sure!' she protested. 'I…'

'My getting into bed with you was not the brightest notion I've ever had,' he abruptly decided, cutting through what she was saying, his back to her. And as, stunned, she watched, she saw him grabbing up his trousers and begin to get into them.

Disbelieving, she stared at him. Disbelieving but, as it started to sink in that she had to believe it, she had to accept it. Erin could only be grateful for pride, that chose that moment to storm in. While wanting to desperately beg him to come back to her, she thanked heaven for pride that won the day and stated she would see him in hell before she would beg.

'Well, pardon me for being undesirable!' Pride alone pushed the huffy words out between her teeth.

'Even with your small experience, you know better than that,' Josh clipped, his shirt on, buttoning it up as he went. 'Get dressed and go home,' he ordered—and gave her the solitude to do just that.

Erin was too upset to think of hurling something at the door after him. How could he leave her like this? After awakening her body the way he had—how could he possibly leave her?

CHAPTER FIVE

ERIN arrived at her place of work on Monday fully intending to resign from her job. She got as far as going to see Ivan Kelly. 'Ivan…' she began, but found that the words to sever even the most remote possibility of seeing Josh again just would not leave her lips. 'About that Pickering query…' she went on, and on the spot asked him about a problem that she had already dealt with.

With the memory of how she had been with Josh beginning to haunt her, Erin drove to Croom Babbington on Friday evening wondering if she would ever stop feeling hot all over with embarrassment about that particular subject. Talk about giving him the green light to go, go, go! For goodness' sake, the 'Take me, I'm yours' sign must have been flashing in brilliant neon!

She felt quite shocked whenever she thought of her behaviour, her reactions. No, not even *re*actions. Because she'd been the one pushing for his kisses—all the way. Trollop? Forward? My stars, she had given the poor man little alternative but to kiss her. He had probably only kissed her anyway because he couldn't shut her up any other way.

Erin tried to get angry—against him. That didn't work either. She tried to tell herself he should never have got into bed with her in the first place. What sort of thing was that to do? Even if he *had* been sitting talking to her for a couple of hours to keep her awake—and then spent another couple of hours watching her sleep. Prior to that, no doubt yawning and bored to death, he had looked at that larger portion of free space on that bed and had thought—hang it. The fact, though, that he had carried her to that room and had so diligently watched over her weakened any anger she tried to drum up. No wonder he had given in to the notion to share what in any case had been his bed to start with!

Erin sighed heavily, knowing that, aside from what she considered was her wanton behaviour, what was really the most humiliating thing of all was that Josh Salsbury should so easily reject her—um—charms. Oh, he had desired her; she knew that well enough. But she recalled how he had curtly informed her that time he'd driven her home from the office, 'Some men might want to bed you, Erin Tunnicliffe—I'm not one of them.' His actions in the early hours of Sunday had clearly borne that out. It was without question that he certainly hadn't desired her enough to want to 'bed' her last Sunday.

She had hoped that a weekend spent in quiet and uneventful Croom Babbington might give her some peace of mind. It did not. 'See you next weekend,' she said cheerfully when on Sunday, with every appearance of being light-hearted, she bade her father goodbye.

'Drive carefully,' he instructed, which she did, automatically, her head once more filled with thoughts of Josh Salsbury.

With Josh dominating her thoughts so much, however, she arrived in London and took a phone call from her mother that gave her pause to consider that perhaps she was not the only member of her family going through, as it were, 'the emotional mill'.

'Have a good weekend?' Nina enquired.

'I went to stay with Dad.'

'What you'll do for laughs!' her mother offered sarcastically.

Erin did not want to get into the sort of conversation where her mother maligned her father and left her feeling she had to defend him. 'How did your weekend go?' she asked.

'Well…' Nina began, but hesitated.

'Anything the matter?' Erin queried, realising suddenly that her mother's tone was a touch subdued.

'Nothing. Nothing at all!' her parent answered briskly. 'I just thought I'd ring and suggest we meet somewhere for lunch tomorrow.'

There *was* something troubling her! Erin just knew it. 'Fine,' she answered, wanting to press to find out what the problem was but knowing from her mother's 'Nothing' reply that she would have to wait until tomorrow to find out what it was. 'Same place as last time?'

'It's as good as anywhere,' Nina agreed. 'I've nothing else pressing tomorrow. I'll come and pick you up.'

'I'm working, Mother.'

'I know! I know!' Nina plainly objected to any hidden suggestion that she had forgotten. 'And less of the "Mother". I meant I'll come and pick you up from your office.'

Erin was not at all happy with that. 'You do know I work for Thomas Salsbury's company?' she dared to further remind her.

'Well, I'm not likely to run into him, am I? The last I heard he wasn't even in London but abroad somewhere, convalescing in some place sunny. Not that I'd mind running into Tommy; he was always good company. Up until he proposed, anyway.'

'It wasn't him I was thinking of,' Erin had to confess.

'Oh—you think his son might be around and attempt to give me a talking to for daring to turn his father down?'

Erin wasn't sure what she thought, other than, Murphy's law being what it was, and even knowing the likelihood of bumping into Josh was highly unlikely, if she *were* to bump into him then for sure Murphy would arrange it for tomorrow.

'He wouldn't dare,' she answered lightly. 'But I think it would be more tactful if I meet you there.'

Her parent did not mind either way. But with their arrangements made she rang off, leaving Erin to wonder what tomorrow's lunch was all about, but glad she was going to meet her away from her place of work. Unlikely though it was that Josh would be around at lunchtime tomorrow, Erin was sure he'd be bound to have something to say should he see her mother.

The next morning, bearing in mind that the lunch she'd shared with Mark Prentice had overrun into her office time, and with her mother having 'nothing else pressing' that she had to hurry for and knowing she would not see any urgency to have lunch over and done with in an hour, Erin went to see Ivan Kelly.

'Any problem if I extend my lunch hour today?' she asked.

'Lucky man,' Ivan fished.

'My mother,' Erin obliged. 'A half-hour extra should do it.'

'Consider it granted.' They exchanged cheerful smiles and Erin went back to her desk.

With something else to think about, albeit Josh was never very far away from her thoughts, Erin started to believe that she was getting over the humiliation of the wedding weekend.

Her mother was at the restaurant first, a clear sign she must have something on her mind, Erin mused as she joined her.

'Darling, you're much too pretty to have to work for a living,' Nina greeted her. 'Get your father to increase your allowance.' She instantly countermanded that. 'Though since you're much too soft to get what is only rightfully yours from him, I'll speak to him on the subject myself.'

'Honestly M—Nina, you're the end,' Erin commented, but had to laugh. 'I don't need Dad's money. My bank balance is more than healthy.'

'Is it?' Her mother seemed surprised, then, her tone sharpening, 'You're not getting miserly like him, I hope?'

Whatever her father was, he was not miserly. He had always been generous where money was concerned. And Erin knew for a fact that Nina had walked away from her marriage to him with a settlement that would make most men's eyes water.

So she glanced across at her mother, looking absolutely as lovely as ever, and began to realise that all this was a smokescreen to hide something that must be troubling her greatly.

She became more and more certain of it when her parent kept up a lively light-hearted chatter all the way through their first course. But when their second course arrived, and her mother appeared to have nothing more deep to talk about than her latest shopping exploits, Erin guessed that there was a man involved somewhere.

'How's—Richard?' Erin asked, bringing to the surface the name of her mother's last beau—the one Nina had declared was 'different'.

'Ah!' she exclaimed, and Erin knew she had struck a nerve.

'He's—still making you laugh?' she probed gently.

Nina gave a heartfelt sigh. 'He's gone all serious—

you know the way they do,' she complained. 'He's ruined everything!'

'You've finished with him?' Erin asked, unsure whom to feel more sorry for—Richard or her scared-of-commitment mother.

'I'm... He proposed. Honestly, I've avoided proposals like the plague for years, and then two—one on top of the other! Anyhow, Richard has asked me to marry him. Can you believe that? When I'm sure I made it perfectly plain to him that marriage and me don't agree!'

'But—I thought you—cared for him?'

Nina gave her an unsmiling look. 'I do,' she admitted. 'But I've tried being married. Twice!' Her tone lightened. 'I'm just not ready for it,' she said, her unsmiling expression giving way to such an endearing impish grin that Erin could quite see why so many men fell for her. Nina's grin had disappeared, though, when she went on to casually enquire, 'I suppose you're going to stay with your father this coming weekend?'

'He likes me to go home when I can.'

'He's a selfish old devil,' Nina announced crossly. 'Tell him you've got your own life to lead.'

'I didn't go down to Croom Babbington the other weekend...' Erin began to defend, then, as light shone through, 'You want me to go somewhere with you this coming weekend?' she guessed. But even as the words left her lips she was realising the absurdity of that. Her mother loved her, but had never craved her company for a whole weekend—ever.

But, to her astonishment, 'Funny you should ask,' Nina replied. 'But I wouldn't mind if you paid me a visit on Saturday—and stayed overnight.'

'What sort of trouble are you in?' Erin quickly asked,

certain that only in the direst of consequences would her mother need her under her pantiles.

'Not trouble, exactly.' Nina shrugged prettily. 'The thing is, I need space—space to think, to decide...'

'And you haven't got that?'

Nina shook her head. 'Some weeks ago I arranged for Richard to join me for this coming weekend so he should take part in some charity swimathon in Norman and Letty Ashmore's pool. Can you image it?' she broke off to insert. 'Half of them are heart attacks waiting to happen.' Erin inwardly winced. That was the fate Josh's father had suffered. But her mother went unthinkingly on, 'Anyhow, some bright spark suggested a six a.m. dive-in, and with more wine than judgement we all agreed.'

'You're swimming too?' Erin asked—foolishly, she realised the moment the words were out. Her bandbox fresh mother was averse to water on her face, and that was without so much as dwelling on what chlorinated water might do to her hair.

'No, darling,' her mother reproved mildly. 'What I am doing, or did when everyone said they'd meet at the Ashmores' for five-thirty—which would mean Richard getting up at some unearthly hour to drive down and be in Berkshire in time—was to offer him a bed at my place for Saturday night.'

'Which he accepted?'

'And which I can't now take back or he'll think the worst of me, not to mention the spoilsport I shall look in front of the others. Oh, why did he have to go and ruin everything yesterday by asking me to marry him?'

'You said—no?' Erin asked, trying to keep up.

'Richard could see I was about to, and quickly suggested I thought deeply about it before I gave him my answer.'

'And you agreed to do that?'

'Weak of me, but I said I would.'

'Only, until you've made your decision you don't want to be too much alone with him this coming weekend?'

'I think I've half decided.'

'You're going to turn him down?'

'I think Richard has to be the first to know my decision,' Nina replied, showing the delicacy of nature that Erin had known she possessed.

'You're sure you want me there?'

'It's essential! You'll come?'

'Of course,' Erin answered unhesitatingly. But, half to herself, 'I only hope I don't slip up and call you Mother.'

'Richard knows I have a daughter.'

Erin looked at her parent in amazement. 'You told him!'

'He caught me at a weak moment,' Nina confessed, but went on briskly, 'No one else need know—you needn't come to this charity thing. Richard can go on his own as it's so early. I can drive over to the Ashmores' later.' Neatly avoiding spending time solely in Richard's company, Erin gathered. But her mother's tone was altering again when she went on, a touch despondently, 'Though, come to think of it, I don't think I particularly care so much now who knows that I've a grown daughter.'

Erin recognised that her mother must be in something of the same emotional turmoil that she herself was in. Which then brought to Erin's mind the reason why she was having such an emotional time, and, having thought of Josh, Erin was back in her own emotional purgatory.

It also reminded her of her place of work. She glanced at her watch. 'It's half past two already!' she exclaimed disbelievingly. 'I'd better try and get a taxi back to the office. Do you mind if I skip dessert?'

'I won't bother either,' Nina replied.

It was two forty-five when they stood on the pavement, waiting to flag down a seemingly non-existent taxi. Erin suggested that her mother leave her to wait alone, but perhaps because Erin had so willingly accepted and answered her SOS she declined the suggestion. But, having seldom waited for anything, Nina was soon impatient.

'This is ridiculous!' she announced abruptly. 'I haven't done anything wrong!' And, in a tone that said there was no arguing about it, 'Come on, I'll drive you back.'

Erin went with her to where Nina had parked her car, supposing that in Nina's eyes she had *not* done anything wrong with regard to Thomas Salsbury. Nor did Erin have any idea of what had gone on between her mother and Josh's father. But something had triggered his heart attack, and it was for certain that not many men would walk away from the rejection of a sincere proposal of marriage without feeling a little stressed about it.

'What time shall I arrive on Saturday?' Erin asked as her mother confidently threaded her smart car through traffic.

'Early afternoon, I should think. I'll get Richard to pick you up. He lives only about a mile from you. It's senseless to take two cars when he lives so near.'

From that Erin gleaned that her mother had it all worked out. By asking Richard to call for her daughter it did away with him arriving early at Nina's Berkshire home. And, since Erin would need transport home, Nina would not be left alone with him after she had gone.

All of which made Erin realise what a dreadfully unhappy time her mother must be going through just now. She supposed that following a refusal it would normally be something along the lines of Perhaps it would be better if we did not meet again. Only this time it seemed her mother was fond enough of Richard not to want to cut off all links with him. Yet at the same time she was afraid of being alone with him in case she weakened from her resolve to never marry again—to actually be persuaded by Richard to say yes.

By the time they were pulling up outside the large imposing building of Salsbury Engineering Systems Erin's feelings were so wrapped up with what her mother must be going through at the moment that she even forgot about the unwritten Murphy's law. The law that said if you really, really didn't want something to happen then you could bet your life that it would. And suddenly—while her mother halted the car and was confirming that she would expect her with Richard on Saturday—Erin froze. Because there, briefcase in hand, strode Josh Salsbury, out through the plate glass doors of the Salsbury building, his long legs making short work of the steps.

Perhaps he won't see me, Erin prayed as joy entered her heart to see him again and mortification jumped on it when, with the speed of light, she simultaneously recalled how totally his for the taking she had been the last time she had seen him.

Not see her! Small hope. Thanks, Murphy! The car was facing him, and Josh looked straight at her. Oddly, for the briefest moment, she thought as he paused and looked at her that he appeared pleased to see her so unexpectedly. He even seemed as if he might come over to speak to her. Then he glanced to the driver's side of the car and an instant look of disbelief swiped away any pleased look. His expression darkened, and was followed by a look so instantly furious, instantly murderous, that Erin knew he had recognised Nina—the woman who had played some part in his father's close brush with death.

Luckily her mother was half turned to her and had not spotted him. 'Bye, darling,' she was saying with a smile, while leaning a little towards her to air-kiss her cheek.

Unable to live with Josh looking as though he would like to do the pair of them the greatest harm, Erin, feeling utterly numb, her brain seized up, turned helplessly towards her mother. When she turned to the front again it was to know that Josh had strode straight on past.

'Until Saturday,' she said to Nina, and with Josh's look of pure murderous outrage burned into her memory she stepped from the car, waved goodbye to her mother, and took a shortcut through the main building and out through the other side to the building where she had her office.

But so upset was she by that murderous look she would have forgotten to apologise to Ivan Kelly for the extension she'd taken on her already extended lunch hour had he not come looking for her, saying, 'Good, you're back.'

'I'm sorry. I lost all track of time,' she apologised.

'Not to worry. Though I've a report I need typing. It will probably take you some time.'

'I don't mind working late,' she offered, but when he had gone started to wonder if she would still have a job at Salsbury Engineering Systems at the end of the day in which to work late at. Somehow, effortlessly recalling

Josh's look of sheer fury on recognising her mother, Erin had a feeling that he had been much too incensed to merely shrug away the fact that his bed companion of just over a week ago was cohorting with a woman he had reason to detest. Somehow Erin had a feeling that Josh striding furiously on was not the end of the matter.

She tried to lose the feeling by scolding—don't be ridiculous, as if he'd bother! For heaven's sake, he'd had a briefcase with him; clearly he had other things on his mind. Other more important things. What on earth did she think a man as busy as Josh would do? Call her up to his office when he got back in order to let forth about whom she should and should not exchange air-kisses with? Wake up!

Nevertheless, Erin was on edge all the rest of the afternoon, and totally apprehensive when, as happened frequently, she was called upon to answer the internal phone.

She worked until just gone six, when the report was finished and ready for a meeting Ivan was conducting at nine-fifteen the following day. She went home and made herself some tea, and wondered why it was that when the threat of her being summoned up to the top floor hadn't happened she should still feel all uptight and tense—as if still expecting something to happen.

She knew why when, as she was standing at the sink rinsing through the dishes she had used, she saw from the kitchen window a car enter the courtyard. It was still light enough for her to recognise it. Oh, help!

Pulling back from the window, she swiftly dried her hands. With her mind in a whirl she dodged into her sitting room and for quite a minute was a complete emotional riot. She had still not got herself together when in the next minute someone, probably with an angry stride to have got there so quickly, was ringing her doorbell.

She would have quite liked not to answer it. But some things had to be faced. Erin took a shaky breath, and after some seconds went down the narrow staircase to open the door to Josh Salsbury.

Hot colour surged to her cheeks the moment she saw him. Mortification and embarrassment were again there to haunt her at how his for the taking she had been the last time she had seen him—and at how he had declined the offer.

But, as she had suspected, he was still angry about seeing her and the companion she'd been with after lunch, still murderously furious. She could see it in the fire of his eyes. She was not mistaken, she soon discovered. His hostility was rife as unspeakingly he eyed her for about two seconds before, it becoming plain he was in no mood to bother with pleasantries, he snarled harshly, 'I don't think much of the company you keep!'

On that instant her embarrassment fled. She had spent an apprehensive afternoon knowing somehow that she would be hearing something from him—most likely dismissal from the firm—without doubt he would find some good business reason for throwing her out. But the fact that he had come to her home, and was all too obviously dead set on insulting her mother, was more than flesh and blood could stand.

Erin was glad to feel angry, but did not care to trade insults on her doorstep. Without a word she turned from him and marched back up the stairs to the sitting room.

Josh Salsbury did not wait for an invitation. She heard the outer door close none too gently, and heard his footsteps as he followed her up the stairs. It was but a few seconds after that that he was in the room with her and they were angrily facing each other. Erin didn't know how she could be so angry with him when she loved him so much—but perhaps that was all part and parcel of loving someone—it made you sensitive to the smallest slight. Only this wasn't some small slight. This was her mother he was talking about.

'You seem very friendly with her!' Josh bit, when Erin had not yet said a word. No doubt he was referring to their air-kisses on parting. Still she wasn't saying a word. That was until, his jaw jutting, 'How do you know *that* woman?' he demanded.

That woman! That woman was her mother! Erin raised her head a proud fraction, and then fairly hurled at him, 'Since you're obviously desperate to know—that woman...' Erin paused to take an indignant breath '...is *my mother!*'

That shook him; she could see that it had. Whatever he had been expecting it certainly hadn't been that. Erin saw his brow shoot back as, speechless for a moment, he stared at her. But he was not speechless for long.

'She doesn't have any children!' he contradicted harshly.

Sorry, Mother, I forgot. 'Correction. She has a daughter!'

'She has a different last name from you.'

My stars, he was intent on digging and digging, by the sound of it. 'My mother remarried after she and my father divorced,' Erin stayed civil to inform him coldly.

'And became Woodward,' he documented, clearly having her name seared into his memory. 'Or was Woodward husband three or four?' he questioned with cutting sarcasm.

'Two. My mother now has an aversion to the married state.'

'She should have told my father that before she proceeded to make a fool of him!' he barked.

'She probably did tell him,' Erin defended.

'So how come he was so completely floored by her rejection?' Josh demanded grimly. 'How come he was so flattened by her turning him down—not what he'd been led to expect at all—that he made himself ill?' And, not waiting for an answer, but becoming more incensed than ever, *'You knew!'* he accused. 'All this while you've known about it!' Her anger with him began to fade, guilt banishing it. 'You've lied to me!' he charged hostilely.

'No, I haven't!' she denied, glad of a small flurry of anger.

'I specifically asked you if you knew my father,' he carried on antagonistically, as if she had not spoken. 'You told me no.'

'I don't know him!' she protested.

'You lied by omission. You know of him. You knew he'd asked that woman to marry him. That she so heartlessly spurned him. You've known all along!'

'It wasn't...'

'What a terrific time you and your tramp of a mother must have had. A whole barrel full of laughs at the expense of my father!' he fired, outraged, more outraged still as he added, 'And of me.'

'I've never laughed at you!' Erin denied hotly. 'And don't you *dare* call my mother a tramp!'

'Why not? She doesn't care whose heart she breaks!' He broke off, looked racked for a moment—Erin guessed he was thinking of his dear father—but then came roaring back to life, hurling at her, 'Like mother, like daughter! Hell's teeth, was I taken in by you!'

'What do you mean?' Erin questioned faintly.

'What *would* I mean? All that virtuous talk of never having been to bed with a man! All that play-acting,' he jibed. 'The innocence, the shyness, the nervousness. It didn't last long, though, did it—once I got you between the sheets?'

'Are you being deliberately offensive?' she challenged, angry but with no defence, and she knew it. Shyness had played only a very small part once Josh had started to kiss her.

'Offensive?' he mocked. 'You were so willing. Had my tastes not run in other directions I could have had you any time I liked.' And, his words and tone deliberately insulting, 'I still could. You, like your mother, are anybody's!'

Erin sucked in her breath. His words were meant to wound, and wound they had. He had desired her, she knew that he had, but his tastes, as he'd just said, lay in other—probably more sophisticated—areas.

'My mother's not like that!' she defended as best she could. But in all honesty didn't know what her mother was like in that direction. 'And you're wrong about me!' Erin informed him heatedly, raising her head proudly. Love him she might, but she did not have to take this.

Though as a glint of something she did not quite understand came into his eyes, she was soon to know that her words and the proud look of her had been received by him as a challenge. 'Wrong, am I?' he thundered angrily.

'You know you are,' she insisted.

'Joke of the day!' he sneered. 'You're denying you were so all fired up in that bed that you told me not to dare to stop?'

'You're—um—taking it out of context!' she protested, a familiar feeling of humiliation about her behaviour that early morning getting to her again.

Josh shook his head and came nearer. 'It doesn't take much to turn you on, does it, little Miss-butter-wouldn't-melt-Tunnicliffe?' he drawled, his anger still there, his control hanging by a thread.

He took another step closer—Erin started to get worried. 'I think it's time you left!' she ordered crisply.

'Oh, you do?' he mocked.

'Right now!' she demanded, taking a step back as he came another step nearer.

'When I'm ready,' he retorted ominously.

'N-now would be a good time.' She was by then seriously worried, and took another step back. And another. It was a small room, and as Josh continued to come relentlessly forward so suddenly Erin's retreat was halted when her back came abruptly up against a solid wall.

'Go!' she ordered hoarsely. He smiled. It was a smile that had no humour in it. Oh, heavens.

He came closer. 'Wrong, am I?' His tone was silky, and suddenly there was no doubt in Erin's mind that, while he might prefer a more sophisticated woman in his bed, he was angry enough in his belief that she had played him for a fool, furious enough on his father's behalf and his own, to take up her challenge and prove that she would be his any time he cared to take her.

'I shall fight you!' she stated, her violet eyes worried, huge in her face as she strove for courage.

But apparently he welcomed a fight. 'Good,' he replied. 'That should make it more interesting.'

She looked wildly about, wondering if she could make it out of the room and down the stairs and outside before he caught her.

He read her mind to answer. 'No chance.'

She tried to bolt anyway. He caught her before she had taken two steps. 'No!' she yelled, but he was strong, much stronger than her, and he was pulling her back, pulling her into his arms.

'You'll soon be saying yes,' he assured her confidently, pinning her flailing arms at her sides as his head started to come nearer.

His mouth fastened over hers. *'No!'* she screeched, dragging her mouth away from his.

He smiled. 'This must be a new role for you, sweetie—playing hard to get. Especially when you know and I know that that's all it is, play-acting.'

'Get lost!' she snorted, and aimed a kick at his shin which, as she heard him grunt, connected. But she gained only small satisfaction from that because, more incensed, he made his arms rigid around her, making it impossible for her to free herself.

His head came down again and his mouth was over her mouth, forcing her lips apart. She wriggled, she struggled, she kicked at his shin again, more viciously this time. It connected. 'I'll soon settle you!' he grunted, obviously believing he had taken enough of that because, while she was still struggling furiously, he did no more than take her kicking feet from under her by picking her up in his arms.

'What...?' she gasped as he began to carry her from the room.

'I think I know somewhere we'll both be more comfortable,' he informed her, staring malevolently down into her bewildered face.

But she was not bewildered for long, because suddenly she knew what he was about. Stunned, she stopped fighting—for about two seconds. Then, one arm free as he carried her to the bedroom, she was punching and pummelling at him and generally fighting like a tigress to be free.

And was free—briefly. That was because Josh allowed her to be free when he tossed her down on the bed. Winded, she struggled to rapidly get up. But, as swiftly as she had moved, he was not wasting a moment either. And before she could leap from the bed he had found the perfect way to keep her where he wanted her.

'Get off me!' she shrieked when he lay down on top of her, using his body to pin her down.

'Trying to pretend you don't like it?' he mocked.

'Go to hell!'

He smiled an insincere smile. 'Don't be like that,' he coaxed.

'I hate you!' she spat.

'Preferable to your love, sweetheart,' he retorted, entirely unmoved, and aimed a kiss at her mouth, which met her cheek when she jerked her head away. He then proceeded to kiss her throat, one hand free as he unbuttoned her shirt and kissed her throat.

Infuriated, Erin used her body to try and jerk free, her lower torso coming into solid contact with his hard male body. 'Will you get off…?' she demanded.

He mockingly cut her off. 'Oh, sweetie, do that some more and we'll have a fine time.' And then his mouth was over hers again, seeking, taking—and Erin, in love with him still, while hating him for what he was putting her through, did not want these sort of kisses. When before they had lain on a bed together his lips, while seeking, had been giving and not all taking. Had been tender and sensitive to her, not punishing and so totally insensitive.

She wrenched her mouth away from his. 'Don't…'

was all she could manage before he claimed her mouth again in another angry kiss.

And that was when it suddenly came to Erin that to fight him was not the way to go about it. Josh wanted her opposing him, fighting him—it fuelled his anger. But if she lay passive, unresisting, would he then leave her? She knew a little of him by then, had socialised with him—if you could call it that—had worked for him, and thought that she knew a little of his sensitivity.

She stopped moving. Stopped writhing beneath him. By then she was fully aware that he wanted her, that his body desired her body—but she did not want him—not like this—in hate.

The next time his mouth clamped on hers she let him kiss her. When he forced her lips apart she let him. He raised his head, his expression saying What's this? Unsmiling, she met his gaze. He caught on. 'You think passive resistance will stop me?' he demanded harshly.

She shrugged her shoulders. 'I don't expect you to change your mind about what you intend to do to me,' she answered quietly. 'I'm just a bit surprised, that's all.'

He looked for a moment as if he would resume his onslaught of her regardless, but then hesitated. 'Surprised?' he questioned.

She smiled up at him, her voice taking on a taunting note. 'Correct me if I'm wrong, but aren't you the man who once told me, and I quote, ''Some men might want to bed you—I'm not one of them''?' She could still feel the pressure of his maleness against her, and further taunted, 'Surely you haven't changed your mind and now want to bed me after all?'

Josh Salsbury raised himself away from her, an inscrutable kind of look in his grey eyes. Somehow she managed to stay perfectly still, just doing that taking all of her will power. And then, to her relief, Josh at long last rolled away from her.

Unmoving, she eyed him, but could tell he was still hating her. Or the person he still thought was her. Because his tone was cutting when he coldly reminded her of something *she* had once said, his arrogant tone beating her taunting one hollow when he loftily told her, 'I sure as hell don't want to marry you, sweetheart!' With that he got up from the bed.

She could, she supposed, have attempted to retaliate with some kind of acid remark. But as she watched him leave, for all she had won, she felt too beaten to try.

CHAPTER SIX

THAT night, the night after he had gone, seemed endless. Erin was still going over and over Josh's visit at three the next morning. No wonder she had decided not to tell him that the woman who had broken his father's heart—in more ways than one—was her mother. Look what had happened when Josh had found out!

Feeling mentally bruised and battered, Erin turned restlessly over yet again in her bed. She had known he would be angry, furious even, but in all honesty had she deserved such treatment?

Dawn eventually came into being and she left her bed knowing that deep down she would always love him—unfortunately love could not be turned off just like that, no matter how one might desire it. She was glad, though, to find as she went to shower that her pride had surfaced and come to her aid. She had spent a good deal of last week in mortified embarrassment at how eager to be his she had been. But no more!

She hoped she had last night shown Josh Salsbury that it was untrue and that she was not, as he had accused, anybody's. She refused to dwell on the fact that had he kissed her in any way tenderly, as if he did not hate her, the outcome might well have been different. But while acknowledging that she loved him she hated him too, that he could treat her the way he had, no matter what the provocation. And she was just not going to put up with it.

And, being of that mind, as soon as she arrived at her

office Erin went and sought out Ivan Kelly. She handed in her resignation. From choice she would have preferred to leave straight away. But there was always masses of paperwork in the experimental division, and she liked everyone there, and loyalty to her particular group meant that she was honour-bound to give them a month in which to find her replacement.

'You can't leave!' Ivan protested. And, as intelligent as she knew him to be, 'Was that where you were yesterday? At a job interview?'

'I had lunch with my mother, as I said. I haven't got another job lined up yet.'

'Then stay until you have. Or—is there something you're unhappy with here? Tell me what it is,' he urged. 'Whatever it is, I'm sure I can put it right.'

If only he could. She shook her head. She was unhappy, in fact had never felt so down, so beaten, but there was nothing Ivan or anybody else could do about that. 'It's a domestic matter,' she told Ivan, and liked him more than ever when he respected her privacy and did not press her further.

Domestic? Erin went home that night having spent the day hiding her inner unhappiness and feelings of near despair. And once inside the walls of the small mews apartment she almost gave way to tears. But she would not give way. Pride kicked in once more; no man was worth it.

Her pride was still riding high, indignation joining it that any man should push her to this pitch, when suddenly her phone rang. She did not feel like answering it, but if it were her father it would be a chance to let him know that she would not be paying Croom Babbington a visit at the weekend.

It was not her father but—astonishingly—Josh Salsbury!

'I…' he began, and, oddly for him, seemed at a loss for words. But to give that weird notion a hiding he was going on to inform her, 'I'm in New York.'

Erin was too winded for the moment to be able to answer. Then her pride surged anew and she was suddenly furiously angry that he thought he could ring her and verbally insult her over the phone into the bargain.

'I'll see you when I get back…' he was saying.

It was as far as she allowed him to get. 'Not if I see you first, you won't!' she hurled at him, and slammed the phone violently down—wishing it had been on his head.

Tears sprang to her eyes then. No! No! No! She would *not* cry! How *dared* he phone her? Who the devil did he think he was? The fact that he'd rung her home number decreed it was nothing to do with work. And if it was personal—as in 'You, like your mother, are anybody's'—then she'd put up with more than enough of that, thank you very much.

Erin went to bed unhappy and got up unhappy, and went to work determining that she was just not going to let Josh Salsbury do this to her. So when Stephen Dobbs stopped by her office and asked her to go out with him that evening, she pinned a bright smile on her face and said she'd love to.

She slept badly that night, and was not any happier when that evening's paper, purchased so she should look at the Situations Vacant column, showed a picture of a dinner-jacketed Joshua Salsbury squiring some New York lovely around.

She hated him, hated her—the woman with him—but that did not prevent her from cutting the picture out of the paper. The male half of it anyway. She placed it in her bedside table, telling herself she'd buy a set of darts tomorrow and use the picture for target practice. She forgot all about scrutinising the Situations Vacant column.

Erin had a difficult telephone conversation with her father the next evening. It was just acceptable to him that she would not be driving to see him this coming weekend, but totally unacceptable that she should be driving to stay the weekend with her mother. Erin thought it politic not to tell him that, to be more precise, her mother's friend Richard would be doing the driving. Not that Nina would give a hoot what she told him.

When around nine that evening her phone, which seldom rang, again let her know that there was someone waiting to speak to her, Erin owned to feeling nervous to answer it.

Thanks to pride, and a determination that no man was going to reduce her to this, she picked up the offending instrument and managed what would pass for a civilised, if curt, 'Yes?' down the phone.

'Erin?'

'Yes,' she answered, more affably this time. It was not Josh Salsbury—she began to wonder why she'd thought it might be.

'Greg Williams,' her caller announced himself.

Just what she did not need! 'Hello, Greg. How are you?'

'Better now I've reached you. How are you now? Apparently you went out like a light when you connected with that pillar.'

'I'm fine, thank you,' she replied, hoping that if he had rung to ask after her health then he would now go.

Too much to hope for! 'I've only just this minute managed to track down your phone number.' She waited politely for him to say why he wanted her phone number, and he went on, 'Our plans for the other Saturday went up in smoke, didn't they? But I'd like to see you again.'

Erin went hot all over when she recalled how his plans for the other Saturday had not coincided with her plans, and how Josh Salsbury—more experienced than she—had so much sooner than her clearly seen what had been in Greg's mind. It suddenly struck her that perhaps the way, in her ignorance, she had been with Greg had gone some way to concrete in Josh's mind that she was, indeed, anybody's.

'I'm sorry, Greg,' she said abruptly—she'd had enough of this. 'I knocked myself out before I had a chance to tell you, but I never had any intention of being more than just friends with you.' And, in case he still hadn't got the message, 'I just don't—do not—sleep around.'

Something of a lengthy pause followed her terse statement. But she came close to liking him again when at last he gave a dramatic sigh and commented, 'Win some, lose some,' which made her laugh, and went on to state, 'I sometimes come up to London; perhaps I could ring you one weekend?' He made her laugh again when he said, rather tongue in cheek, she thought, 'We could go to the zoo or something.'

As if! She couldn't see him spending any time strolling round a zoo. But he had lightened her mood and she was glad of that. 'Ring me then,' she invited, though doubted, since she spent the weekends out of London, that she would be there if he rang.

Inside minutes of that phone call ending Josh Salsbury was back in her head. Though this time, while still out of sorts over him, Erin found she did not hate him so much as she had.

Erin had an overnight bag packed and was ready when Richard Percival arrived to drive her to her mother's Berkshire home on Saturday. He was a good-looking man, perhaps two or three years older than Joshua Salsbury—stop thinking about him, do—and Erin liked him on sight.

'Nina tells me you work for Salsbury Engineering,' he commented as they drove along.

So much for putting a block on Salsbury-type thoughts! 'Do you know the firm?' she asked politely.

'Only by reputation—which, as you know, is first class.'

It pleased her that Josh's firm had a first-class reputation, but this wasn't helping her to forget him. 'What sort of work do you do?' she asked Richard, eager to get away from anything to do with the Salsbury name.

Having liked Richard on sight, she grew to really warm to him during the next twenty-four hours. While it was true that he did not wear his heart on his sleeve, so to speak, Erin saw the way his eyes followed Nina around the room, and it was clear to Erin that he was deeply in love with her mother.

Just as it was equally clear that her mother was most anxious not to be left alone with him. Which in turn caused Erin some small embarrassment, because while Nina's manners were as ever perfect, and she treated Richard as a much wanted guest in her home, if Erin slipped out of the room for any reason she would find that within half a minute her mother had made some excuse and had slipped out of the room too.

'You're going to have to have a private conversation with Richard at some time,' Erin said when, returning a tea tray with cups and saucers to the kitchen, her mother had followed to help.

'Stay close,' Nina said sharply—and then Richard was there too.

'Anyone fancy a walk?' he enquired.

Erin, while quite liking the idea of stretching her legs, was aware the invitation was meant for her mother, and was about to decline the suggestion when she caught the frantic signals her mother was making.

'Lovely idea.' Erin took up Richard's suggestion and, certain that he was nobody's fool and knew exactly what was going on, felt sure that she was the more embarrassed of the three of them.

Knowing that Richard had only suggested a walk in order to spend some time alone with the woman he had given his heart to, Erin was even more embarrassed when her mother declined to accompany them.

'We don't have to go far,' Erin remarked, feeling quite awkward about it as she and Richard started out.

'Nonsense. It will do us good. I've been desk-bound too this week,' he answered cheerfully. His cheerful tone had departed five minutes later, however, when he enquired, 'Has Nina mentioned that I've asked her to marry me?'

Oh, grief. A proposal of marriage should be private, between two people, particularly if, as might be in this case, the suitor got turned down. 'Er…' she faltered.

'Sorry. That wasn't fair,' Richard apologised, and Erin warmed to him some more for his sensitivity. 'New question,' he went on. 'How would you feel were I lucky enough to become your stepfather?' Oh, Richard, please don't count your chickens, Erin fretted. 'You wouldn't be averse to the idea?' he pressed.

No, she wouldn't. He was a nice man, a good man, and, having seen the way he regarded her parent, Erin felt they would do well together. 'I just want my mother to be happy,' she answered, and hoped that Richard would know that, had she been averse to the idea, she would not have encouraged his suit to her mother by accepting this build-up to any step-relationship by taking a walk with him.

'And would you say your mother is happy with me?' he continued to press.

Nina *was* happy with him; Erin knew that she was. She also knew that her mother was scared stiff of entering a third marriage which she might or might not want to get out of in a few years' time. Erin searched for something positive to reply, and found it in, 'Nina says you make her laugh.'

'Well, that's encouraging,' he replied. Then he smiled and promised, 'I give you my word, I won't say another word on the subject.'

Erin stayed home the next morning, though she was aware that Richard was up and about early. She was no lie-abed either, and had showered and dressed and had joined her equally early rising mother downstairs by seven.

'I suppose I'd better get myself over to the Ashmores',' was her mother's greeting. And, getting straight to what she wanted to know, 'What did you and Richard talk about on your walk yesterday?'

'You should have come with us,' Erin answered.

'Are you being cheeky?'

'Am I being reprimanded?' They both laughed, and Erin revealed, while feeling a tinge disloyal to Richard, 'We spoke of marriage proposals. One in particular.'

'He still has this notion he wants to marry me?' Nina asked sharply.

'You know he has.'

'Oh, Lord!' Erin feared the worst. Her mother did not

look very happy about it. 'I'd better go. I shall never hear the last of it if I'm not there for the mutual back-slapping.' And, back to being her more usually effervescent parent, 'Thank heavens they'll all be out of the water and dressed. I've seen their skinny, varicosed, knobbly-kneed legs before—not a pretty sight.' She laughed, and a short while later was leaving to drive the small distance to her friends the Ashmores.

Erin's thoughts were soon centred back on the man whom on Tuesday she had hated and whom today she wished she still did. 'I'll see you when I get back,' he had said, and her heart gave a little flutter at the thought. It steadied down again when she recalled her furious, 'Not if I see you first, you won't.' She doubted she would see him after that. Though that did not stop her wondering why he had phoned—from North America, no less—to tell her that. From what she knew of him, wasn't it more likely that he would just turn up if he felt like doing so? And—her ridiculous heart just did not know when it was beaten and fluttered again—why would he want to see her again anyway? If it was merely to give a repeat performance of his last visit, then, thank you, but no thanks.

And if he had no intention of calling at the mews apartment ever again, but was stating his intention of seeing her at her place of work, then he'd better get himself back here from New York within the next three weeks. She had already served one week of her month's notice.

Her mother and Richard were having something to eat over at the Ashmores' house, so Erin made herself some lunch with her thoughts still on Joshua Salsbury and his phone call from New York. She guessed that he made phone calls from abroad like most people made local telephone calls, so saw no special significance in the fact that he had bothered to call her from so far away.

But why would he bother to make even a local call to her? she had to wonder. Was he intending to make contact to further insult her? She recalled his voice had sounded more sort of carefully even than anything.

Had he tried hard for that even tone? Had he been afraid that he might lose control and lambast her from New York with whatever it was he had rung up to castigate her about?

Thoughts on the fact that the only things he could censure her about was her mother's behaviour in relation to his father and what Josh believed to be her own loose-moralled behaviour kept Erin fully occupied.

Shortly after three, earlier than she had anticipated, her mother drove up, closely followed by Richard in his car. Her mother did not wait for him, but entered the house straight away.

'How did the swimming go?' Erin asked Richard when he came in.

'To the devil with modesty,' he said with a smile. 'You're looking at a champion.'

Erin beamed a smile back at him as she congratulated him. But she sensed a slight tension in the air and was sure she wasn't imagining it. Particularly when he declined her mother's offer of some tea.

Sensitive to atmosphere, even if both her mother and Richard were too well-mannered to be anything but pleasant to each other with a third person there, Erin sensed that now would be a good time to leave.

'Any time you want to make tracks back to London?' she suggested.

'I do have some important work I should be doing,' Richard answered. 'We could go now, if you're ready.'

Within half an hour they were on the road. Richard regaled her with an amusing account of the swimathon as they drove along. But the nearer they got to London the more he seemed unable to keep up the pretence that all was well with his world.

There was sometimes difficulty in the mews courtyard if other mews-dwellers were entertaining Sunday visitors, as was the case when Richard went to drive through the archway. At once assessing the situation, he reversed out from the archway and found a nearby parking spot.

Erin would have collected her overnight bag and said goodbye to him there, but he insisted on carrying her bag to her door. 'Would you like some tea?' She felt courtesy demanded it after his drive—besides, she liked him.

He shook his head, dropping her bag down by her door. 'I'll get off.' He smiled then as he looked at her. 'I should have been proud had I been allowed to claim you as my stepdaughter,' he said quietly, pain in his eyes that he could not totally disguise.

'Oh, Richard,' Erin said softly. 'Did my mother…?'

'The lady said no.'

'I'm so sorry,' Erin said sadly, a hand going to his arm in genuine sympathy.

He took a step back. 'I doubt our paths will cross again,' he commented. On impulse he came forward again, and this time put his arms round her and gave her a hug in parting.

'Bye, Richard,' she said, and, aware that no words of hers were going to ease his pain, stretched up and kissed his cheek.

'Bye,' he answered.

Erin felt quite choked as she watched him walk away. Poor Richard. He must have managed to get her mother on her own at some time after all. She felt sorry for her mother too, because if her mother followed her usual pattern she would now, whatever her feelings for Richard, refuse to see him ever again. He knew it too. It had all been there in that 'I doubt our paths will cross again.'

Erin turned to the door, inserted her key in the lock and turned it. But with the door open she was startled almost out of her skin when from nowhere an all-masculine hand was there, picking up her overnight bag and tossing it indoors. And as he straightened, looking none too friendly, Erin stared at him stupefied. *Josh!*

'Who was he?' he snarled before she had her breath back.

Where had he sprung from? 'The wanderer returns!' she snapped, remembering that last time she had seen him and not feeling very friendly either. She would not be pleased to see him; she would *not!*

'Who?' Josh demanded.

She ignored his question, but took quite some pleasure in being able to tell him, 'If you've made a special journey especially to dismiss me, then you can't! I've already handed in my resignation and leave in three weeks' time.'

He did not look impressed. 'This has nothing to do with business!' he rapped. That being the case, Erin stepped over her threshold. So too did Josh. Deliberately—and with more force than was required, in her opinion—he slammed the door shut and in something of a fury again demanded, 'Who was he?'

By then, although starting to come away from the shock of seeing Josh—an angry Josh—so unexpectedly, Erin was still stunned enough to be on the way to forgetting that someone by the name of Richard had driven her home.

'Who?' she questioned snappily back.

'Don't play smart with me!' Josh Salsbury gritted.

Who did he think he was? She looked up into grey eyes that were threatening and her heart started to pound. He was close, too close. There just wasn't room for two angry people in this space at the bottom of the stairs that could not in anyone's wildest imaginings be termed a hallway.

Erin turned away, needing some space, and started up the stairs. 'You know your way out!' she lobbed arrogantly at him over her shoulder.

A mistake!

Josh was right there with her when she reached the top of the stairs, a hand descending on her shoulder spinning her round to face him. 'Don't you turn your back on me!' he ordered her furiously.

Oh, my word! Erin knew she was in trouble. But she discovered she had too much spirit to do what she knew she ought to do—perhaps apologise and answer anything he wanted to know. 'Correct me if I'm wrong, but haven't we been here before?' The murderous look in his eyes made her quail, but still her tongue wouldn't shut up. 'Isn't this the part where you pick me up and throw me on the bed?'

As if burnt, he thrust her away from him, pushing past her to go to the sitting room. She knew, she supposed, that if she decided to go back down those stairs and out of the apartment this time she would probably make it. But she still loved the bad-tempered swine—and love, and a need to be with him, no matter what the consequences, was in charge of her.

She did what her head said was wrong. She followed

him to the sitting room. Josh had his back to her, but although she had entered without making a noise he must either have sensed she was there or have heard some small sound. He turned to face her, saying nothing, just looking his fill.

He took what seemed a steadying breath, and, with his glance fixed determinedly on the stubborn look of her, he asked, 'Who was he?' with no let-up on his insistence to know.

'It doesn't matter who he was. I shan't be seeing him again.'

Josh took that on board. 'That was one very tender parting of the ways!' he sneered.

'What?' She'd lost him somewhere.

'Have you been with him all weekend?' Josh demanded, his tone more quiet than it had been—Erin felt it to be more ominous.

She could, she supposed, have told him that both she and Richard had been staying with her mother. That Richard had been her mother's man-friend. But a sensitivity to Josh's father rose up just then and prevented Erin from telling Josh where she had been—and that her mother had just dumped another one. His father apart, Josh's opinion of her mother was already low—she did not want it going any lower.

'Well?' Josh demanded, obviously believing he had been waiting long enough.

'Yes,' she answered, her chin tilting even as she saw his jaw clench at her affirmative answer. 'I've been with him ever since he called for me yesterday.'

'So you've finally done it!' Josh grated, his quiet tone straining at the leash.

Erin did not mistake his meaning. 'I thought you regarded me as some kind of tramp!' she reminded him hostilely. 'But it has nothing to do with you, anyway, whether I did or didn't!' she snapped, going red in spite of herself. And wanting to get away from the subject, she found she was repeating, 'I won't be seeing him again.'

'So either you did, and didn't care very much for the experience, or you didn't and he got upset that his hopes for the weekend got ruined. Which was it?'

Erin was starting to get angry again. Honestly! This man! This man—he thought he could barge his way in and be privy to the most intimate details of her life!

'It's none of your—'

'*Did* you bed him?' he cut in.

'I've seriously had enough of you!' Erin tossed at him shortly.

'You did!'

'As if I'd kiss and tell!' Erin jibed, close to hating one Joshua Salsbury once more. 'What's it to you anyway?'

'Not one damn thing!' he roared, not taking kindly to her attitude. And, coming close enough for her to be able to see flecks of amber in his grey eyes, 'I'm just the idiot who declined to take what you were so clearly offering when you clung on to me in my bed!'

She hit him. She didn't mean to. She didn't even know that she was going to. She just did. Saw red and her right hand flew through the air and caught him a furious blow. *Crack!* His head jerked to one side and she was on the instant totally appalled and ashamed. Violence was just not part of her nature. Or—she hadn't thought it was. Being in love was making a nonsense of everything she had thought she knew about herself.

'I'm sorry!' She rushed to apologise at once, her voice hoarse with emotion. 'I didn't mean to... You just...'

She turned her back on him. Regardless that he did not care for her turning her back on him she turned away, unable to bear the look of utter fury in his face.

Half expecting to receive some similar kind of retribution, she just stood there waiting—nowhere to run to. But then, to her complete surprise, two hands came to her arms. Not harsh and biting, as she would have expected, but gentle, almost tender.

'You're trembling,' Josh said somewhere above her bent head.

'I used to be a perfectly sane, rational person before I met you,' she said, entirely without thinking. Then, realising what she had said was much too revealing, 'You barge your way in here—' strictly speaking that wasn't true '—make aspersions about my friendship with Richard—' She broke off when she felt herself being gradually turned about.

'Richard being the one you've just denied visiting rights?' Dumbly she nodded, fearing to raise her head for what, in this weak moment for her, Josh might see in her eyes. 'So if you're friends do I take it you're not lovers?'

She was back in love with Josh in this gentle, more tender mood. She felt she could hold back nothing from him. 'I'm truly sorry I hit you,' she apologised again.

'And you and the surplus-to-requirements Richard were never lovers?' Josh placed a hand under her chin and began tilting her face upward so he could see into her eyes.

But only when she felt she had control of herself did Erin allow herself to look straight into his eyes.

'We never were,' she admitted.

Josh smiled. 'And Stephen?' he enquired. 'Did you make Stephen redundant too?'

Stephen? Oh, Stephen Dobbs. Erin vaguely recalled that time she had been working directly for Josh and Stephen Dobbs had rung through and she'd said she would see him the following Monday or something. 'I'm—er—still seeing Stephen,' she answered truthfully, but oddly didn't think her answer had gone down well. Perhaps Josh did not care for staff fraternising after work. But she didn't want Josh going back to the brute he had been. 'Forgive me,' she said softly, and stretched up and kissed the spot where her furious hand had connected. 'If it's any consolation, I think I've broken my hand.'

Josh groaned. 'What am I going to do with you?' He caught hold of her right hand and laid his lips on the palm. Then, looking at her, he smiled. 'That's both of us kissed better,' he murmured—and for ageless seconds they just looked at each other.

It was without haste then, giving her all the time in the world to pull away, should she so desire, that Josh took her into his arms. And Erin had not the smallest desire to resist. It seemed light years since she had last seen him. She wanted his arms around her. She did what she wanted to do—she rested her head against his chest. And Josh seemed strangely content to hold her tenderly to him, one arm moving, his hand coming to her shining blonde head.

Gently he stroked her hair, and she wanted to stay like this for ever. But that age-old fear that Josh might catch a glimpse of her very deep feelings for him began to stir, and although it took a deal of effort of will she pulled away from him.

His hold on her slackened, just that alone telling her that she was free, that he would not hold her against her will. She fell in love with him all over again. 'I—er...'

She tried for sense, but the most sensible thing she could think to say was, 'I'd better ring my father. I told him I'd ring when I got back.'

Josh looked a touch amused. 'You want to do that right now?'

Well, as a matter of fact, no. Perhaps her eyes gave away that sentiment; she hoped not. But, as gently as before, Josh began drawing her to him again. This time she did not rest her head on his chest, but was ready and waiting when Josh gently kissed her.

'Oh,' she said on a breath of sound as their kiss broke and she looked up at him.

He laughed lightly. 'Oh—more? Or, oh—that's enough?'

She laughed too. This was totally ridiculous. 'Perhaps just one more—er—purely to make up for my dreadful temper when I hit you.'

'I earned it,' he absolved her. But grinned spine-meltingly when he added, 'Though perhaps one kiss would make it less painful.'

'Does it still hurt?' she asked in alarm.

'Not at all,' he replied, and if he was lying she never found out, because his head was coming nearer and once more he was claiming her lips.

And they shared more than just one kiss, his kisses absolving him too in her eyes for those other kisses taken, not given, the last time they had been together.

Her heart was drumming wildly and she neither knew nor cared where their kisses were leading. She enjoyed, adored his gentle caresses, his kisses to her throat. He unfastened her shirt and placed tender kisses on her silken skin, moving her shirt and bra straps aside as he tasted the sweetness of her shoulders.

Oh, Josh, Josh, Josh! His touch was magic. Her arms

were around him, joy taking her just to hold him. They kissed again, a kiss that hinted that soon there would be no going back. Erin did not care—she was on fire for him. She wanted to make love with him—she rather supposed that he knew that too. She pressed her scantily covered breasts against him, and was enthralled when his hands on her hips drew her to him.

'Josh, I...' she choked.

'Scared?' he asked, his eyes serious on her eyes.

'No,' she answered honestly. But laughed shyly as she confessed, 'Adventurous.'

He smiled at her. 'It's quite something of an adventure.'

'I—er—um...' She swallowed hard. 'I—think—I'm ready for it.'

He kissed her in delight. 'You have to be sure you are, not think you are, little darling,' he suggested softly—but she was too enamoured of him to be able to think logically. 'It's a big step.'

She knew that it was. But he was her one and only—and she wanted his lovemaking to remember when he had gone. But she hesitated. Was she being too forward? She wanted to die from the shame of it. 'I'm too eager?' she questioned.

He smiled. 'No, love. You've just waited for a long time—and one of us has to be sure that the time is now.'

'You're not sure—about you?' Oh, grief! The moment the words were out Erin realised that they sounded as if she was asking for some kind of commitment from him. Without thinking further, she pulled out of his arms and, taking a step or two away from him, felt herself colour when she saw the disarray of her clothes. Hurriedly she buttoned herself up. 'You'd better go,' she mumbled.

'Is this nerves speaking?' Josh asked, not coming after

her but giving her all the space she seemed to need just then.

'How would I know?' she answered, more snappily than she'd meant to—had Josh no idea of what he had been, and was still doing to her? 'I've never b-been this—um—far before with any man…' her voice faded, the 'but you' never said.

'Oh, Erin,' Josh said softly. 'Come back to me.'

She looked at him and was undecided. He must not know of her love for him, but oh, how she ached to be back in his arms. 'You're asking?' she questioned guardedly.

He did not hesitate. 'I'm asking,' he replied, and smiled a welcome.

'In that case,' she murmured, and went to him, loving him, exchanging kisses with him again, her emotions once more out of control, her body soon on fire for him again.

Josh took her to the sofa, their bodies pressed closely together when suddenly the phone started to shrill for attention. They both tried to ignore it—it declined to be ignored. Josh put some daylight between their two bodies. 'This is impossible,' he grunted. They both sat up.

Erin could not agree with him more. 'It might be my father,' she guessed. 'He'll ring and ring. I'd better answer it. Oh, grief.' She went a pretty shade of pink.

'Oh, grief, as in…?'

'As in, What were you doing that it took you so long to come to the phone?'

Josh grinned wickedly, and Erin, her emotions all over the place, hurried from the sofa, straightening her clothing as she went. It was not her father—but Greg Williams! Oh, heck.

'Oh, hello, Greg.' She answered his greeting, watched

Josh's grin disappear, saw his mouth tighten as he got up from the sofa and went to stare out of the window. 'Er—how are you?'

'Glad that at last I've managed to find you in. I've been ringing your number since yesterday afternoon!'

'I'm sorry.' She apologised nicely for not being there, though in fact her thoughts were more with Josh than the man she was speaking with. Which made it a total nonsense that, when she had been at pains to make no reference to her mother in Josh's presence, she should go headlong into explaining to Greg, 'I've been staying overnight at my mother's place.'

She looked hastily at Josh—his shoulders were rigid, and Erin knew right then that she could forget any thought of sharing more kisses with him. He turned, and there was that in his eyes that said he had remembered his father and what her mother had done to him. Erin looked away. Without doubt Josh was not too happy to realise that his lovemaking with Nina Woodward's daughter could be construed as disloyalty to his father.

Erin tried to focus on what Greg was saying—something to the effect that he had wangled a day off work next Thursday and how was she fixed to see him if he came to London?

She had not the smallest wish to see Greg Williams again. Against that, however, she was quickly realising that she was someone who had bedroom experience only with Josh—that experience indisputably unfulfilled—and Josh must, with his experience of women, have gained some clue that she cared more for him than any man she knew. Hadn't she only just told him that she had never been 'this far' with any man? It was time, she realised, to let Josh know that she was not enamoured of him to the exclusion of all men.

'... shall I?' Greg Williams was asking.

'I'd love to see you Thursday,' she answered. Josh's jaw jutted. She did not care—he must not know that the sun rose and set for her in him. 'I'll see if I can get some time off too. Let me have your phone number. I'll give you a call and we can finalise details.'

'Great!' Greg exclaimed enthusiastically, gave her his phone number and would have gone on talking at length had not Erin, trying not to show she was affected in any way by Josh's glowering expression, told Greg that she had company and now was not a good time to chat. 'I'll look forward to your call,' he told her, and eventually rang off.

Erin put the phone down, her heart aching. She could tell from the icy expression on Josh's face that they were going precisely nowhere. She supposed, despite those rapturous moments of mutual ardour, that she had always known that. They never had been.

'Impossible, did I say?' Josh questioned curtly. 'Totally bloody impossible, I should have said,' he gritted, and added icily, 'You shouldn't have terminated your call on my account—your company's leaving!'

Again Erin had cause to be thankful for her pride. Her heart might be bruised, sore and bleeding—but she still had her pride. 'Do allow me to show you out,' she offered sweetly. But could have done without his look of utter disgust as he passed and, denying her the pleasure of closing the door after him, strode angrily out, down the stairs and closed the outer door behind him with a quite dreadful thud of finality.

CHAPTER SEVEN

ERIN wished she could get thoughts of Josh out of her head. But thoughts of him haunted her after he had gone. She tried to think of something else, something other than him, and succeeded for about two seconds. Then Josh was back again.

She ejected him once more and decided to ring her father, as she had promised she would. But found she was in such an agitated stew over Josh Salsbury that she was just not yet ready to speak to anyone.

A half-hour later her father rang her. 'Been back long?' he enquired.

'Not too long. I intended to ring you.'

'Did you have a good stay with your mother?'

Erin was sensitive to her father's feelings, but felt that it was all right to truthfully tell him, 'We had a very pleasant time.'

'Who's she going around with now?'

Difficult territory. Erin wondered for all her parents' regularly exchanged insults if her father still felt something for his ex-wife. 'Mother isn't seeing anyone at the moment,' Erin glad to once more be truthful, was able to tell him.

'My God, the sky will fall in!' he exclaimed sarcastically.

'How was your weekend?' Erin changed the subject matter.

'Hmm...' Her father hesitating? Erin was intrigued. And even more so when he revealed, 'Actually, the woman who moved into the old Raven place about a month ago invited a few neighbours in for a drink last night.'

Erin could not believe that he had accepted. From what she knew of her father she would have said, if asked, that he would run a mile away from such invitations. 'You—went?' she asked.

'I thought I would.'

Just that! Erin decided it was time to use a daughter's prying privileges. 'What's her husband like?' she asked casually.

'Brenda's a widow.' Brenda! First-name terms! Not Mrs So-and-so, as with his other neighbours—but Brenda! 'Actually,' Leslie Tunnicliffe was going on, 'it occurred to me that as she's new to the area it might—um—well, perhaps we should invite her to dinner one Saturday.'

Grief! This was a sensational departure! It even put Josh Salsbury to the back of Erin's mind for longer than a few seconds. 'I'll be home this Friday,' she replied quickly, sensing her father was feeling a bit off-footed with this conversation. 'Would this Saturday be too soon?'

'I'll think about it,' he replied, but Erin did not miss that there was a smile in his voice.

While that phone call had given her something else to think about, Josh was soon dominant in her head after her father's call was ended. Josh had called her 'little darling', he had called her 'love', and she wanted him back with her—but the finality in the way he had closed the door clearly showed that he would never call again.

She escaped that harsh reality by dreamily recalling those lost moments in his arms. She thought of his wonderful kisses, his gentleness, his tenderness with her—and wanted that time back again.

But rushing in came the memory of how Greg Williams's phone call had changed all that. She had mentioned her mother and that was all he had needed. Josh had turned icy. Impossible, he'd said—he was right there.

By nine that night all Erin wanted to do was to go to bed, pull the covers up over her head and hope for oblivion until morning.

No chance! Logic told her she must have slept at some time, but it did not feel like it. She was up early on Monday, having spent half the night going over every word, look and nuance that had passed between her and Josh Salsbury from the moment she had first met him that morning when he had joined her and Charlotte for a cup of coffee.

Erin showered and dressed with Josh refusing to budge from her head. In the end she admitted defeat and let him stay, and tried to dull the incessant ache by being angry. What right had he to come knocking on her door anyway? Not that he'd bothered ringing her doorbell yesterday. He had simply been there and had taken the liberty not to wait for an invitation to come in. Though, come to think of it, he had probably realised after the previous episode that he'd have had a long wait for that sort of an invitation.

But why come at all? And had he just arrived at the same time as she and Richard, or had he been there waiting for her to come home? Huh! She scoffed at the notion that he might have been waiting for her—they didn't have that sort of relationship, or any other sort of relationship, for that matter.

While she accepted that she and Josh were more personal than employer and employee—my stars, were they—Erin recalled her state of undress yesterday and went hot all over. Too much had gone on between them. She had slept with him—albeit in the purest sense—albeit not from her choice—so very definitely they were positively more personal than employer and employee should ever be.

All the same, in her view they still did not have the sort of 'thing' going where Josh Salsbury could just pop over to the mews apartment any time he felt like it. And she'd jolly well tell him that the next time he… Her thoughts faltered. She remembered his icy parting words, the way he had looked just before he had left. That awful thud of finality as he'd shut the door on his way out—and she knew indelibly then that she would not see him again.

She felt defeated, and the hour being early, no need to rush around prior to leaving for the office, she went over to the sofa. She sat there for quite some while and hoped never to be this unhappy again as she came to terms with love and life, and the fact that she could not go on like this.

Then the phone rang. And she jumped. And she thought of Josh, her pulses racing for all she knew that it would not be him. Was this how it was going to be? That she would think it was Josh on the other end of the phone every time it rang?

It was not him; it was her mother. 'Good morning, darling!' Nina greeted her brightly. 'I thought I'd get you before you left for the office. I wonder if you're free for lunch today?'

'Of course,' Erin answered equally brightly. 'Same place?'

'If you like,' Nina trilled, and rang off. And Erin went

back to her contemplation, knowing that she was not going to have to ask Ivan for an extended lunch hour—because she was going to ring him shortly and terminate her last link with Joshua Salsbury.

She would find it not an easy task. But she knew that it was the only thing she could do. She must cut Josh completely out of her life. He wouldn't give a tuppenny damn about it, of course. In all probability he wouldn't even know that she no longer worked for him. But while she was anywhere near that building Erin just knew that she would be constantly, and fruitlessly, hoping to catch some glimpse of him.

A little after nine, while she was still of the same mind, Erin picked up the phone and dialled. She did not think she would weaken, but she felt in such an emotional turmoil that she did not trust herself not to have second thoughts.

'Oh, Erin, you can't leave just like that!' Ivan Kelly protested when she had explained that due to unforeseen domestic complications she was unable to work out her notice as she had hoped. 'Perhaps our human resources department can help?' he suggested. 'They're very good, and extremely discreet if—'

Feeling worse than ever, Erin hurriedly cut him off. 'No, no. Thank you all the same. I've so enjoyed working with you, Ivan, but…'

Ivan had lived long enough to understand that some matters just could not be put right with the help of outside agencies, no matter how good those agencies were. And they ended their business relationship with Ivan asking her to promise to be in touch should her present difficulties be resolved, when he would be happy to re-employ her.

Erin came away from the phone, glad that she had

done what she had done, but not feeling the slightest bit better for it. Ivan had been a love about her leaving him in the lurch like that, and she felt dreadful and ashamed. But what else could she have done? She did not want to go to an office so close to where Josh worked. Was she to spend the next three weeks sitting at her desk hoping he might have business in her section? Was she to wander the corridors of the main building hoping to catch a glimpse of him? No. It had to end now. And she had ended it. So why did she feel so miserable and so at rock bottom?

Erin pinned a smile on her face when she went to meet her mother. And as lunch progressed she began to realise that her mother's own bright smile was hiding that Nina was not feeling so very full of the joys of spring either.

'I've—er—finished with Richard,' she mentioned casually. 'Pass the tartare.'

Erin passed her mother the sauce to go with the fish she had ordered. 'So Richard mentioned.'

'He told you?' Nina asked sharply, the tartare sauce forgotten. 'What did he say?'

'Just that he would have been proud to have me as his stepdaughter, but that you'd said no.'

'Was he upset?'

'Oh, Mother, of course he was upset.' That he was not the only one who was upset was evidenced for Erin in that her parent let the 'Mother' go by without rebuke. 'You're going to miss him, aren't you?' she asked gently.

Her mother gave a long sigh. 'I am already,' she admitted. 'And it's not twenty-four hours yet! He didn't ring last night, or this morning.'

'Um—did you expect him to?'

Nina sighed again. 'I suppose not. And I'd have been very cross if he had,' she bridled, though was sounding quite fed-up when she added, 'But I'm going to miss those telephone calls.'

It seemed to Erin, who was enduring a love problem of her own—one that could not be resolved—that all her mother had to do to make it right was to pick up the phone and call Richard. She dared to say as much.

'I know I haven't been married, and can't possibly know how horrid it must be when a marriage fails, but—would it be such a terrible thing for you to marry Richard?'

'Make a third marriage, you mean?'

At least her mother wasn't biting her head off. Erin grew a little bolder. 'Well, to be honest, it seems potty to me that when you care for Richard, and he cares for you, you should both be so unhappy to be apart when there's something you can do about it.'

'But—marriage? I've tried it twice, remember?'

'Yes, but with the experience you have surely...?'

'I couldn't possibly go through another divorce!'

'You're looking at it from the wrong end!' Erin protested. 'Would you, right now, prefer never to see Richard again?'

Her mother didn't answer that question, though Erin noticed she did not look very cheerful at the prospect of never seeing him again. 'Men get so dull once you're married to them,' she complained. Then smiled, the old Nina not submerged for long. 'I'm just not ready to settle for a life of "What's on TV tonight, dear", and some man being king of the remote!'

Erin laughed; her mother was impossible. 'From what I've seen of Richard, I'd say he'd very likely give you your own remote as a wedding present.'

'See what I mean—hum-drum city.'

All Erin saw was that she was losing the argument and that her attempts to make her mother see that she could feel happier were failing miserably. 'Have you told Richard how you feel? How, for all you don't show it, you're still carrying mental scars, baggage, from your previous failed marriages?'

'It's nothing to do with him!' Nina bridled again. And, looking at her lovely daughter, advised her sharply, 'And you're much too observant for your own good!'

What I am, Mother, is in love as well, and finding it extremely emotionally battering. 'I don't want you to be unhappy,' she said gently. 'Why not ring Richard? Open up to him. Tell him—'

'I'll tell him what I think fit to tell him!' Nina broke in to retort sniffily. But Erin was pleased to note that she had not declined outright to ring him.

By the time she and her mother parted company they were friends again. And Erin went back to the mews apartment with much to think over. Josh was in her head again, of course—he seemed to go everywhere with her. But when she was able to concentrate on her mother Erin only hoped she was not feeling so downcast as she was feeling. Erin did so hope not, particularly when she knew that there was every chance her mother could do something about it. All she had to do was to ring Richard, start talking and…

Josh was back in Erin's head. He had not been away long. Were it Josh, Erin knew she would ring him. Though Richard loved her mother, and Josh…

Fat chance. Erin knew Josh had desired her on a couple of occasions, but he was a virile male—and desire wasn't love.

She made a pot of tea around seven. But, unable to

settle with a book, decided, sternly, to get her act together. She was still sitting there at eight, her thoughts having darted all over the place. Firstly she had started off by determining what to do with her future—but had lost some time when Josh, her mother, Richard, her father and the unknown Brenda had claimed a helping of her thoughts, Josh taking the lion's portion. Then she'd thought about work and how she would get another job. Then Josh and her family had intruded again, until all at once it had dawned on her that there was not the smallest need for her to stay on in London. She could work anywhere, for that matter.

Erin gave brief thought to returning to Croom Babbington to live. She loved her father, and she knew he would welcome her back, but somehow, having left home, having tasted something different these past months, Erin knew, with no disrespect to her father, that she did not want to return to Croom Babbington. What she wanted to do was to stay in London.

She was just about to analyse that when her phone rang. Josh? Ridiculous! As was proved when, with her heart pounding, she answered it.

'Are you all right, Erin?' It was Stephen Dobbs, sounding most concerned. 'I've only just got in—one of those Mondays! Ivan mentioned just as I was leaving that you'd rung in to say you wouldn't be coming back. He wouldn't say why. Is it anything...?'

'It's—er—a domestic matter.' She fell back on that excuse. Stephen was now more friend than work colleague, but still the same Erin did not feel able to confide about her inner emotions to him.

'Anything I can help you with?' he offered at once, like the good soul he was.

'No. I can cope,' she declined.

'Are you able to come for a drink one night this week? We could grab a bite to eat somewhere if you like?' he suggested.

Erin was about to ask him if he'd mind leaving it until next week, then flashing into her head came that newspaper picture of Josh, living it up in New York, and her pride once more surfaced. 'I'd like that,' she replied, and arranged to see him on Wednesday.

She had barely ended her call from Stephen, though, when her phone rang again. She knew in advance this time it would not be Josh—that wasn't his way. Present himself in person and then invite himself in—that was his way. Not that that would ever happen again.

So her heart was only moderately pounding when she picked up the phone and said, 'Hello.'

'Your line was engaged,' said a voice guaranteed to have the blood rushing wildly through her veins.

'St-Stephen,' she answered witlessly.

'Stephen?' Josh queried, as she struggled to gather a modicum of composure.

'I'm seeing Stephen Wednesday,' she replied, proof there if proof was needed that her brain matter had taken a hike. 'Er—what...?' She didn't get to finish.

'You're seeing Greg Williams on Thursday,' Josh documented, his voice strangely even. She wondered at that. It was almost as if he were holding himself in check about something.

Ridiculous! This love business was causing her to have the most absurd notions. 'You know how it is,' she said off the top of her head. 'No date for ages then two come along at once.'

There was a pause, but again his voice was even when Josh reminded her, 'You *have* remembered that

Williams's idea of a fun date might not necessarily be the same as your idea of a fun date?'

Oh, Josh. Erin sank down onto the sofa, fearing she might fall. 'Greg—er—knows I'm not—er—like that.'

'Those weren't the messages I was reading the one and only time I saw the two of you together,' Josh stated bluntly, his even tone gone. 'When did you tell him?'

'What?' she answered, not sure she cared for this line of questioning.

'When did you tell him that he was wasting his time—um—coming the—old soldier?'

Erin burst out laughing. In spite of herself, in spite of that feeling of starting to get a tiny bit niggled with Josh, she just had to laugh. Fancy him remembering! 'I told him when he rang previously.'

'You obviously gave him your phone number at Robin and Charlotte's wedding?'

'I didn't, actually,' Erin replied, a smile back in her heart just to be talking with the man she loved. 'I expect he rang Charlotte's parents or something.'

'Just how many would-be lovers do you have?' Josh enquired, to Erin's ears with a kind of tough edge in his voice.

'I don't think—'

'I can think of five straight off,' he stated sharply.

'You know more than me, then!'

'Gavin, Mark...'

'Gavin? Who he?'

'Gavin—the thigh-crusher.'

Gavin Gardner! 'Ah, yes.'

'Richard, Stephen,' Josh went on. 'And, most irrefutably, Greg Williams.'

'I've told you,' Erin began, and then started to get really annoyed. Love him she might—but what was this?

'Just why have you rung, Josh Salsbury?' she demanded crisply.

There was a brief pause, a sort of hesitation, as if her question had come before he was ready for it. Rot, said her head. 'I thought you might like to know—I've got a black eye.'

Her breath sucked in. From where she had hit him? 'You haven't!' she denied, distressed. 'Oh, tell me you haven't!'

There was a pause, and she had to wait an agonising second or two before he agreed, 'No, I haven't.' And, with a smile there somewhere, 'I was just after your sympathy.'

She didn't believe that for a moment. She wished then that she didn't love him, but she did. And, even though she wanted to stay talking with him for as long as he liked, there was a proud part of her that made her question, 'That wasn't why you rang?' knowing full well that once he had told her the reason for his call he would then end it.

'You weren't in work today.'

How had he found that out? 'I—don't work for you any longer,' she told him jerkily.

'So I heard,' he replied quietly. 'May I enquire why?' He needed to ask? 'I thought you said you'd some weeks to go before you left?'

Erin did not wish to invite some third degree, even though she had no idea why he would bother. She had been good at her job, but did not doubt she would soon be replaced with someone equally efficient. Yet she shied away from telling Josh that she had some domestic problem, knowing she would only end up tying herself in knots if, unlike Ivan Kelly, Josh pressed to know more.

'I've—had enough,' she answered at last.

More moments of silence followed while Josh considered her answer. Then, his tone even once more, 'My fault?' he enquired.

Too true it was his fault. 'You said it!' she retorted sharply, seeing no reason to hide that, after his visit yesterday, she had decided she'd had enough.

Though she was totally unprepared for him to dissect her answer and to then come back with a quiet, 'I have that much effect on you, Erin?'

'I—er... I—er...' Totally stumped for an answer, she did the only thing she could do—she came out fighting. 'Look here, Salsbury, I didn't invite you here yesterday. And I didn't invite this phone call either. So you can either state now why you've phoned, so I can get back to what I was doing—' which was precisely nothing '—or I'm going to put this phone down and get myself an ex-directory number!' She felt near to tears. Pig, pig, pig!

Quite a lengthy pause followed, and she thought he must have gone. But still the same she just could not put the phone down—not until she was sure he had gone. Then suddenly, quietly, Josh was saying, 'I grew impatient of waiting.'

'Waiting?'

'You didn't phone.'

She wasn't with him. She wasn't surprised that she hadn't a clue what he was talking about—she was completely all over the place. 'Me?' she questioned.

'You said you would ring me.'

'No, I didn't!' she denied. Lying hound! 'When did I?'

'Don't you remember? Surely you do. We had a date,

you and I, but the day before—a Thursday, I think it was—you rang to say you couldn't make it.'

Oh, yes, of course she remembered. 'It—er—was a Thursday,' she confirmed witlessly. Would she ever forget it? There had been a report in the paper that night about his father suffering a heart attack. Her mother had called and...

'If you remember that, you'll also remember that you had to cancel our date because you were having problems—"a few complications at the moment" I believe you said.' Erin was silent, struck dumb, and Josh waited a few seconds and then further reminded her, 'I suggested that you give me a ring when you had your complications sorted.' He paused. 'Only you haven't rung. And, since that was months ago, I felt sure you must have resolved those complications by now.'

Erin was stunned—and stumped. Was Joshua Salsbury—asking her out? Her heart began to thunder and, quite idiotically, having no answer for him, she put the phone back on its cradle—and terminated the call.

She regretted doing so at once, but then began to wonder if it had been so idiotic after all. Because, while starting to grow certain that Josh had *not* been asking her out, she was also starting to realise that those complications he had reminded her of would never be resolved.

It was a fact that his father had been serious about her mother and that her mother must have encouraged and then rejected him, dropped him, and that Josh's father had shortly afterwards suffered a heart attack. Wasn't that complication enough for anyone?

Yes, but, argued Erin's heart, while she had not then felt able to tell Josh the truth and had hid behind 'complications', he had found out anyway. Yet still he was asking her out? So did that mean that there were no complications? And was he, in fact, asking her out?

She remembered how icy he had gone yesterday when her mother was mentioned. No *way*, Erin decided, was Josh asking her if she was ready yet to go out with him.

Anyhow, she didn't want to go out with him—even if he was offering, which he wasn't. She would never get over him that way.

Feeling too agitated to sit still, Erin got up and went to take a shower. She got into her night things and went back to the sitting room, and was still chewing away at every word of that phone call. Why? Why had he rung? Why? Why? Why?

Was he asking her out? Her heart started to race. She couldn't believe it. But if he *were* asking her out—why? Would Josh ask her out because, well, because he—liked her? Could it be that he did? Oh, she knew well enough that physically they struck sparks off each other, sparks that ignited into a passion of wanting. But she had been his for the taking. He had declined, thank you very much. So why would he bother…?

Was it just that he liked her? Or was it maybe that he was out for some kind of revenge? Did he have some kind of scheme in mind to make her pay for what her mother had done to his father?

Somehow Erin did not want to believe that. But, whether that had anything to do with it or not, she told herself she did not care. She just didn't want to go out with him. He hadn't been asking anyway.

It was far safer to ignore his call, she determined. Safer and, prodded a voice she just did not want to listen to, duller. She went and made herself a cup of coffee. It might keep her awake but she wasn't going to sleep anyway.

Safer and duller dogged her heels as she walked back from the kitchen. She sipped her coffee, finished it, and padded back to the kitchen. She rinsed her cup and saucer and returned to the sitting room, and was then overcome by such a longing to see Josh that she looked over to the phone.

Ridiculous, said her head. He might have said he had grown impatient waiting for her to call him, but he didn't really mean it.

So why had he rung her anyway? The Josh she knew was more likely to present himself at her door, and without waiting to be asked come straight in, before he'd phone.

Erin knew that she would not call him back. But such a feeling of restlessness came over her just then that she got up and started wandering about. In the process she found the telephone numbers Charlotte had given her—Josh's telephone numbers.

Erin went back to the sofa, restless still, safe and dull again bombarding her. She glanced at the clock—close to midnight. She wouldn't ring him. But—why shouldn't she? He was waiting for her call; he'd said so.

She started to feel all hot and bothered, and recalled how only that day she had urged her mother to ring the man she loved. Yes, but this was different.

Erin got up and paced around, the phone seeming to hypnotise her. She couldn't ring him. Yet what was the alternative—to go over and over again on the same treadmill? Safer not to ring him. And duller, prodded the person inside her who had started to decide that if she left it any longer she would have to wait until morning to ring Josh. When who knew where he would be? He was probably always up early and off somewhere. He might even have plans to be at some airport, taking an early flight somewhere.

Her hand hovered near the phone. He might be in bed. So? If he was flying off somewhere at first light was she to wait until he came back—which could be a minimum of a week—to contact him?

But did she want to contact him? Erin sat in deep thought for the next three minutes and then faced that, in all honesty, safer and duller just did not come into it. She wanted to hear his voice, wanted to know why he had phoned. She somehow did not think a man like Josh would just ring to pass the time of day.

And anyway, whether he was in bed by now or whether he wasn't, it was not his sole prerogative to ring people up and disturb them. Not allowing herself to think further, Erin picked up the phone and pressed out his telephone number.

The phone was answered straight away—almost as if Josh was sitting there waiting for her call. Get real! 'Salsbury,' he said evenly, and she couldn't think of a thing to say.

'Er…' was about as much as she could manage.

'I'm glad you rang,' Josh encouraged.

How did he know it was her? Did he know it was her? Perhaps he was glad it was somebody else calling. 'It's Erin,' she said in a rush.

'I know.'

Oh! 'Er—how d-did you know I wasn't in work today?' She had no idea why she had asked him that. She had not intended to.

'I had reason to go to the experimental division,' he answered.

'You never go to the experimental division.' Well, he

never had, not the new place anyway, while she had been there.

'I went today,' he replied, his tone even still, and not impatient as she would have imagined it would be at this nothing kind of conversation.

That word 'impatient' reminded her that he had said he had grown impatient waiting for her to ring. And without further thought she grabbed at what courage she could find, and hurtled headlong in with, 'About our date…' and promptly ran out of steam.

There was an utter deafening silence. Then, 'I'll come over,' Josh said quietly, and, as she had earlier, he put down the phone and terminated the call.

For totally stunned seconds Erin stared at the unresponsive phone in her hand before she placed it back down. 'I'll come over,' Josh had said. When? Tomorrow? She began to feel thoroughly agitated. Tomorrow was Tuesday. He knew that she had arrangements for Wednesday. She was seeing Greg on Thursday. Perhaps Josh would come over on Friday. They had arranged to go out on a Friday before, she remembered—and then suddenly a most astonishing thought just then hit! He didn't mean—*now*, did he? As in, I'll come over—*now?* Erin was on her feet, all at once too stewed up to know what she was doing.

He couldn't have meant that! Surely he couldn't have? Why, it would be about one o'clock before he got here! She was being ridiculous to think such a thing.

Ridiculous or not, and knowing for certain that she was being the biggest fool of all time, Erin went to her bedroom, found fresh underwear, her best trousers and a fine cashmere sweater, and exchanged them for the nightdress and wrap she was wearing.

Grateful that she was the only one who would ever

know what a complete idiot she was being, Erin still the same could not settle or return to the sitting room to wait to have her idiocy proven.

She went to the kitchen but did not turn on the kitchen light. Her view of the courtyard was much better in the dark. Minutes ticked by. After five she went and brushed her hair, only to race to the kitchen window when she thought she heard a car.

There was no car. She waited another ten minutes. She tried to laugh at how ridiculous she was being. Even if Josh had left straight away, which he hadn't, he still wouldn't be here in under…

She caught her breath, almost choked on it, as just then car headlights fanned over her window and a car drove into the courtyard. She recovered, knowing full well that it must be one of the other residents in the mews returning from an evening out.

The car drew to a stop and her breath caught again. It was dark, but she thought she knew the car. A man got out. A tall man. A man of Josh's height.

There was a thundering in her ears as the man walked from the parking area and the security lights came on and caught him fully in their beam as he approached her door. Josh!

Her heart was pounding so hard she thought she might faint. 'I'll come over,' he had said. Not tomorrow, not Friday, but, 'I'll come over—*now*.' And he was here, and she was shaking like a leaf, with no idea of how her legs were going to carry her down the stairs to let him in.

CHAPTER EIGHT

ERIN had still not moved. In fact she felt frozen to the spot when Josh rang the doorbell. She moved then, her head a riot of half-thoughts as she went down the stairs to let him in.

He did not ring a second time, but gave her the moments she sorely needed to get herself under control. Wasted moments. She was still a quivering mass inside as she pulled back the door.

She tried for calm, tried for casual, but he looked—and was—so devastating that all she could do was stare at him. She took a step back. He did not move, but seemed content to just stand there, drinking in his fill of her from where he stood.

That was the moment, that moment of total nonsensical thought, when Erin's brain gave her a prod. 'You don't normally wait to be invited up,' she opened for starters.

Josh stared at her a moment longer before politely informing her, 'It seems to me, Erin Tunnicliffe, that normal flew out of the window on the day I met you.'

She didn't know if that was some kind of joke or what it was. She could find no answer anyway, so settled for a cool, 'You'd better come in.'

Cool—ye gods! She inwardly felt a complete and utter jumble of emotions as she led the way upstairs. They reached the sitting room and she turned to face him, finding it a joy just to have him there. But—why had he come?

'Would you like coffee?' she enquired, like any well brought up hostess would.

'Your father would approve?'

'At close to one in the morning? Probably not,' she replied. 'But let's keep our...' she faltered '...my family out of this. Though...' Abruptly she changed her mind. 'Though that is what this is about, isn't it—m-my mother and your...?' Heavens, she was inviting all-out war! She knew it! 'Do you want to take a seat?'

'Thank you,' Josh answered levelly, but waited until Erin had perched on the one easy chair before taking a seat on the sofa.

'You're being unusually polite,' she said warily, distrustfully, and plunged, 'This visit, you being here, it's all about revenge, isn't it?'

'Revenge?' He looked surprised.

But she wasn't fooled. 'It's the only answer that fits,' she said, as that answer came to her. 'No normal person comes calling at close to one in the morning on account of a—er—an outstanding date.'

Josh looked back at her. 'I may have mentioned that nothing is normal for me any more,' he informed her levelly. But then, as if fearing he had said too much, 'Revenge? What are you talking about?'

She barely knew! He had made it sound as though it was her fault that nothing was normal for him any more. Erin attempted to quieten her racing heartbeats by reminding herself that of course nothing was normal for Josh any more. How could it be? His meeting with her had coincided with his father suffering that heart attack. And although it would have to be his father's lifestyle, work-style, that would probably have to be dramatically adjusted, that adjustment was bound to affect Josh too—hence not normal any more.

'You know what I'm talking about.' Erin pulled herself together to answer Josh's question. 'You believe, rightly or wrongly, that my mother is responsible for your father being ill, and you want me to pay for it.'

Josh looked at her in disbelief. 'You're amazing!' he muttered, and went on to bluntly deny any such notion. 'Complete and utter rot!' he disclaimed.

'Is it?' she challenged.

'Incredible,' he commented. 'To think when you worked in my office for that short time I was so impressed by your quick grasp of matters!'

She tried not to be flattered, and stiffened her backbone. 'Huh!' she scoffed. 'You positively glower whenever my mother's name is mentioned. You—'

'At first, maybe,' he cut in to agree.

'Maybe! Pfff! That wasn't the way I saw it!' She stood her ground.

'So I was furious. Outraged, if you like. But only to start with.'

Erin would like to have done another huff and puff. She had not forgotten how in this very room, only the previous evening, he had changed totally from being a warm and gentle lover to being curt and icy the moment she had made reference to her mother.

She decided to give him more rope. 'Go on,' she invited, 'hang yourself.'

'It's true.' Josh took up the option. 'I was at first infuriated when I saw you in that car with her. Close to exploding when I witnessed you all affectionate to her. This was a woman whose callousness had all but killed my father. I feared for my actions if I was not able to walk on...'

'So you did walk on, and instead you came here. That

night you came here, and—and…' Her voice faded. She could not go on.

'Oh, my dear, dear Erin,' Josh said softly, his tone as much as his words ruining the backbone-stiffening she had thought she had found. 'I've tried to get that dark night out of my head, but cannot. I was so out of control when you told me that Nina Woodward was your mother…' He shook his head. 'Even now I can't believe I tried to force myself on you.'

He seemed much upset at the memory, and despite herself Erin found she loved him enough to not want him upset. 'Y-you thought I was anybody's,' she reminded him.

'As if that excused what I was about!' he said angrily. 'Not that I ever believed that anyway.'

Well, if he could be angry then so could she—she wished she hadn't tried to ease things for him. 'You could have fooled me!' she retorted snappily.

Josh stared at her for some moments, and then confessed, 'I realise now, have known for some time, that the person I was trying to fool the most was me.'

Erin looked back into his dear face. But she was not about to go soft on him a second time. 'Intriguing—if more than a touch totally bewildering,' she retorted sniffily. 'Are you sure you won't have that coffee before you leave?'

He laughed. He actually laughed at her broad hint that he should go. 'Oh, Erin Tunnicliffe, have you a lot to learn about me,' he said, and, his tone mellowing, softening, 'I've built myself up for this moment,' he stated. 'There are—things I need to say to you. Apologies I need to make. Answers that I shan't rest until I know. No way am I leaving until some, most, hopefully all of them have been resolved to my and—hmm—I hope your satisfaction.'

Her throat went dry. Oh, help, she was wilting already! Things to say, apologies to make, answers to his satisfaction—and *hers*, don't forget. 'I—er—I'll—um—take that as a no, then, shall I? Um—about the coffee?'

'Oh, Erin, Erin,' he said. 'Is it any wonder you drive me quite demented?'

Her eyes widened in astonishment. 'Me?' she checked.

He smiled. 'Since you're not running a mile, I'll take courage and explain that I've—' He broke off, as if uncertain if he should go on—how to go on. Then, manfully, he resumed. 'I've been affected by you from the very start, Erin Tunnicliffe, and that's the truth.'

To hear him say such a thing stopped her dead in her tracks, her brain appearing to seize up for seconds on end, until, her lovely violet eyes wider than ever, 'Ph-physically—you mean?' she ventured. 'I mean, I know...'

'Physically, of course,' he agreed. 'That's undeniable. But...' He hesitated, as if selecting his next words. 'It's more than that.'

More than that! Oh, heavens, she was shaking inside, and pushed her hands to her sides down the chair, in case their trembling should give her away. 'I—um—find that statement a bit, well, actually more than a bit, confusing.'

'Open your mind and listen to me,' Josh urged.

Oh, she was listening. Was she ever? 'I'm all ears,' she invited. She could hardly believe he was here, yet he was. Regardless of the hour, Josh, the man she loved, was here, and had stated that he was not going to leave until whatever it was was resolved. 'It has nothing to do with revenge, you said?' she questioned, that to her being about the only clear motive for him being there at all. He surely hadn't left his home at this time of night to come and discuss some proposed date!

'I give you my word, nothing. My father was gravely ill, but is almost back to full health now. I was, as I've agreed, outraged when I knew that Nina Woodward was—is—your mother. But within a very short space of time...'

'When you'd cooled down?' Erin suggested.

He grinned nicely, apologetically. 'I did rather lose it, didn't I?' And, not waiting for an answer, 'I knew full well when I'd cooled down that you were blameless, and that I owed you one very big apology. I rang you from New York to apologise, but...'

'Is that why you rang?' Erin asked, astonished. 'Oh, grief. I didn't give you very much chance, did I?'

'You sounded as mad as hell. Quite rightly too,' he approved. 'I'd behaved despicably. Insulted you with words, let alone brutishly manhandling you. I didn't deserve better. But I knew in any event that a telephoned apology was no way to go about asking your forgiveness.'

'You came in person!' she exclaimed. 'You came yesterday.' Though, since it was now the early hours of Tuesday, 'You came on Sunday,' she corrected.

'I came on Saturday too—when I got in from New York.'

'Saturday?'

'Several times,' he confirmed. 'Even though I knew you'd gone to spend the weekend with your father.'

'Mother, this time,' she murmured, but recalled he knew that from overhearing her speaking with Greg Williams on the phone. Though by then Erin was far more interested, avidly so, in hearing more of what he was so astonishingly saying than in dotting the 'i's and crossing the 't's of which parent she'd stayed overnight with. 'You must have wanted to apologise very much?'

'Apologise—and see you.'

'Ah, see me regarding the apology?' she slotted in. For goodness' sake don't start getting ideas that he was so desperate to see you that he dashed straight to your door from the airport. 'You—came back on Sunday.'

'I was here waiting, when you returned. With Richard,' he added succinctly.

'We'd both stayed Saturday night at my mother's.'

'You take a lot of your boyfriends to weekend with you at your mother's home?'

'I...' She hesitated.

'Be truthful with me, Erin,' Josh requested firmly.

It seemed oddly important to him that she be truthful. So, after a second or two of thought, Erin took a deep breath and said, 'I didn't want to tell you. Not for me, but for my mother.'

'Okay,' he answered slowly as he digested that part. 'Why for your mother?'

'Your opinion of her is already low. I—um—didn't want to give you fuel for despising her more than you do.'

Josh looked solemnly at her. 'I think we both have to agree that whatever has or has not gone on between our parents it must have nothing to do with us,' he said quietly. And her heart, that had been misbehaving for most of the time since she had opened the door to him, started leaping about all over the place again at that 'us'!

'I—er...' she said huskily, and realised she was thinking nonsense. There was no 'us', and any minute now one or other of them was bound to get angry and they'd end up enemies again.

But she did not want that, and what Josh wanted was that she be truthful with him. Though that would mean breaking her mother's confidence. For a few seconds Erin struggled between love and loyalty to her mother, and love and trust for Josh.

She was feeling terribly torn, but in the end, she took one very deep breath and risked, 'My mother has this real and dreadful fear of marriage.' Erin dared a glance at Josh. He wasn't uptight—yet. 'She's been married twice and... Anyhow, she is popular with the opposite sex—she's a fun sort of person.' Erin dared another glance at him. He wasn't looking ecstatic to hear this character reference for the woman who had dropped his father like a hot coal the moment he had proposed, but neither was he looking ready to go for her jugular. 'Nina—she prefers me to call her that—she—um—doesn't much care for her friends to know she has a grown-up daughter.'

'A beautiful grown-up daughter,' Josh inserted, to make Erin's heart go crazy all over again.

'B-but I believe she always makes it clear to any new f-friend that marriage is a no-no.' Erin paused. She looked at Josh. He looked blandly back—she would have loved to know what he was thinking. 'Why am I telling you all this?' she asked.

'Because I need to know.'

'Oh,' she murmured, though was more confused, if anything, by his answer. 'Anyhow,' she resumed, 'occasionally some man will think they know better, and that she doesn't really mean it, and will propose.' Another glance at Josh showed that, whatever his thoughts on the subject of her mother, he was keeping them well hidden. 'Two have attempted to break down her ''never again'' barrier recently.'

'My father,' Josh took up.

'And Richard,' Erin completed.

'Richard!' Josh looked astounded. '*Your* Richard?'

'He was never my Richard.'

'Never?'

Did she see a trace of a smile coming through? 'Never, ever,' Erin answered. 'I hadn't even met him until last Saturday. My mother had by then broken her golden rule and told him she had a daughter. Anyhow, Nina was committed to a charity thing at the weekend that included Richard. By then he had proposed and asked her to think about it. But because she no longer wanted to be alone with him...'

'She invited you to stay too,' Josh took up.

'Richard doesn't live far from here—my mother asked him to call for me on his way.'

'Because she wanted you in her home too, while he was there,' Josh documented. 'So when you said you wouldn't be seeing him again, it wasn't you who ended it but your mother?'

Erin wanted to make more excuses for her mother, maybe tell Josh that perhaps it wasn't the end for her mother and Richard. But Josh being here wasn't to do with her parent or his—her heart did a crazy flutter again—and, although it was too fantastic to be believable, he had used the word 'us'. And, while knowing she was heading for cloud cuckoo land, Erin felt she had explained enough about both her mother and Richard. 'That was one fine way to start off the apology you came to make on Sunday,' Erin mentioned as evenly as she could, recollecting that no sooner had

Richard gone than Josh had been there, demanding to know who Richard was.

'I was a bit—hmm—bad-tempered, wasn't I?' Josh admitted, looking only marginally shame-faced.

Erin wanted to smile, but settled for a simple, 'Why?'

And very nearly collapsed at his answer when, looking her straight in the eyes, he did his own version of drawing a steadying breath and quietly let fall, 'Jealousy.'

'Jealousy!' she exclaimed, her violet eyes huge in her face.

'Jealousy, pure and simple. I was green to the core with it.'

'B-but…' Words failed her.

And she had small chance of regaining her powers of speech either when, sincerely, he went on, 'You, Erin Tunnicliffe, have disturbed me and my peace of mind from the very beginning.'

She stared at him. 'No!' she denied faintly.

'True,' he replied, his grey eyes fixed nowhere but on her. 'I first met you that day you were having a break from shopping with Charlotte. You were seated at a window table when I came by. And I confess I couldn't take my eyes off you.' Erin's eyes were fixed nowhere but on him. 'Then I noticed Charlotte, and before I knew it I, who had only just had a cup of coffee, was joining you.'

'You said you could do with a coffee!'

'How else was I going to get an introduction to the most beautiful woman I have ever seen?'

Erin's mouth fell open. She closed it. Josh thought her the most beautiful woman…

'Oh!' she gasped.

'Exactly. I was bowled over by you. Wanted there and then to ask you out.'

She almost said Oh again, but with a drumming in her ears succeeded in holding it back. 'But—you didn't,' she managed, with what breath his statement had left her.

Josh sent her a wry grin. 'I had a big adjustment to make. I wasn't used to being bowled over. Things like that just didn't happen to me.'

'Mmm,' she murmured, playing for time, terrified of falling into some trap and of maybe revealing more than he should know. 'So you left it a week, and then rang me.'

'And arranged to call for you the following Friday. Only that dinner date didn't happen because you cancelled.'

Erin stared at him, recalling how back then he hadn't sounded in the smallest disappointed when she'd rung him to cancel. But only then did she realise that a man of his sophistication was hardly likely to fall about in a heap to have missed a dinner with someone who, at that time, was virtually a stranger.

'Would I be right in guessing that the complication you spoke of was your mother?' he asked, when she had nothing to say.

Erin nodded. 'I had no idea my mother even knew your father until she dropped in unexpectedly that Thursday. I'd bought an evening paper with the intention of looking for a job,' Erin explained. 'There was a picture of you with your father, tying in with a report that your father had suffered a heart attack. Unusually, my mother stopped by for a few minutes and spotted it. She told me how your father had proposed but that she had—er—felt she had to say no.' Erin tempered what her mother had actually said.

'And you were sensitive enough to see that her turning him down might have contributed in some major way to his heart attack,' Josh concluded gently.

Dumbly, Erin nodded. 'I knew then that I couldn't keep our date—not unless I told you. And had I done so you wouldn't have wanted to keep it anyway. Not without first having a potshot at my mother...'

'And loyalty to her meant you couldn't have that.'

Again Erin nodded. 'I wanted to tell you so many times. Though, to be honest, I had thought several times about ringing you to cancel before my mother turned up that night.'

'You didn't want to come out with me after all?' Josh asked, a frown creasing his brow.

'Not that,' Erin replied quickly. 'I was nervous, I suppose. You—someone like you was quite outside my experience.'

That took his frown away. He even smiled as he commented, 'You don't have a whole heap of experience, do you, sweetheart?' And as her heart pounded anew at his gentle, almost tender use of the word 'sweetheart', he added, 'As I discovered when, you having ditched me for the likes of the drunken Gavin, I found there was something about you—something I must have picked up from the way you were trying to cope in that hotel bar—that suggested you might be in need of assistance.'

'You followed us back here,' she commented. But quickly asked, 'Did you...were you upset that I'd ditched you? Even though I hadn't really,' she added, just as quickly. 'We were never that—um...' Her voice petered out, and Josh took pity on her.

'Close,' he finished for her, but went on to answer her question. 'I don't think I was so upset at being ditched, more fidgeting in my head about you—and quite intrigued,' he admitted. 'You were a new experience to me, so it was no wonder I should have had you on my mind so much.'

She'd been in his head? He had positively lived in hers! 'I was on your mind a little?' she queried—and immediately wished she hadn't fished. But she was discovering that in her love for him she sought every crumb of comfort.

'Oh, Erin, Erin,' he said softly. 'You were on my mind more and more. I should have accepted then what was happening to me—but didn't.'

'Er—what was happening to you?' she asked, that crumb-seeking creature pushing her on to want to know more.

Only for her to stare at him blankly when, quite calmly, quite quietly, Josh replied, 'Oh—I was falling in love.'

'With me?' she squeaked, swallowing hard, not believing her ears, wanting to believe her ears, ashamed of her question and getting abruptly to her feet and turning her back on him. She knew he did not like her to do that, turn her back on him, but she did not want him to see into her eyes. Of course he hadn't been falling in love *with her!* What an utter idiot she was.

Erin stood there, horrendously embarrassed and wishing she was ten thousand miles away—or, failing that, that Josh would just disappear and she might never have to face him again. But he had left his seat, firm hands were on her shoulders, and gently but determinedly those hands were turning her so that she had to face him.

She wouldn't look up. Even when Josh bent his head to hers to quietly say, 'That's why I'm here, Erin, to tell you that I love you,' and a spasm took her, shook her, still she wouldn't look at him.

She could not believe it. And dared not let herself believe it. This was some sort of game he was playing, because… 'It is revenge—vengeance… You said it wasn't, but—'

She broke off when Josh let go of her shoulders and gently gathered her in his arms in a loose hold. 'Forget revenge, forget vengeance,' he urged, giving her a small shake. 'You feel the same love and loyalty to your mother that I feel for my father. But much as we love them, and together, I hope, will deal with future situations, this is about you and me.'

Erin dared to look up then. He held her look steadily, his eyes saying that he was sincere. Oh, heavens—she started to shake. 'You and m-me?' she questioned chokily.

'Us,' Josh confirmed. 'This has nothing to do with anyone but us. You and me.' He took a deep drawn breath, and then confessed, 'I'm here because I've been in a living hell, and after your phone call tonight I just knew I couldn't wait any longer. I knew I just could not spend another wakeful soul-destroying night. I had to find out, now, if I have a chance with you.' A chance with her? 'Oh, sweetheart, you're shaking,' he murmured, and held her that bit closer to him. 'I've come to tell you that I care deeply for you, and…' his voice dipped slightly '…and to find out if there's a chance you might care for me.'

He sounded nervous! Erin couldn't believe what her senses were telling her. She dropped her eyes, but it was no good. She looked up again, straight into his dear grey eyes. He *was* nervous! She was sure of it. Her hands went up to his waist, but whether for his support or her own she knew not.

'You—care for me?' she asked hesitatingly, trying,

daring to try to believe that she was not such an idiot after all.

'I love you with everything that's in me,' Josh declared steadily, going on openly, 'I have, I confess, been in absolute torment over you. How could you possibly love me? I've agonised over how I didn't deserve that you should like me, let alone love me. Had I forgotten how, when pushed on and on, goaded by jealousy, I had shown you a side of me I didn't even know I possessed? How could you love me...?'

'Yet you—th-think I might?' she questioned huskily.

'Not think, hope,' he corrected, the tender light in his eyes threatening to melt her bones. 'I found hope when I recalled your response to our lovemaking in that hotel—but despair when I thought of how vilely I had treated you that day I discovered that Nina Woodward is your mother.'

'Y-you said you were a bit—er—brutish,' she conceded gently.

'Brutish! I wanted locking up!' He tenderly kissed her cheek, and went on to explain, 'I'd thought of you so much that morning that I almost invented an excuse to take a stroll down to Experimental. But, no, I had some of my father's work pressing, and my own diary was overflowing. Besides which, you'd got me in such a state I should probably ignore you, as I did the previous time I'd called in on your division.'

'When we were in the other building?'

Josh nodded. 'Charlotte mentioned in passing that you were now employed by the firm, and...' He smiled slightly. 'I'm not used to women telephoning to break dates with me, so was I going to ring you again? I was not. True, I did pick up the phone a couple of times to do just that...'

'But didn't?' Her heart was in overdrive. She held on to him. He seemed to like it.

'But didn't,' he agreed, firming his hold on her. 'I was a man who liked his freedom. Clearly you did not know the rules. Far better, I told myself, for you to cut your teeth on someone else. Little did I know then that the green-eyed monster was waiting to put me in purgatory should you dare to date anyone else!'

Erin knew a little of that purgatory, and as her faith started to grow that Josh wouldn't be with her here like this, telling her his innermost feelings, unless he meant it, so she felt herself blossoming in his love. Her shaking eased as her confidence took root.

'You came that time to the experimental division to check on matters concerning the move to—' His wry smile caused her to break off.

'Nothing of the sort. I told myself I was coming over to have a few words with the Professor, but, my dear Erin, I later acknowledged that all that had been driving me was a compulsion to see you.' Gently then he touched his lips to hers, and seemed encouraged when she showed no signs of backing away. 'So there am I, when you'd moved into the new building, doing nothing to jeopardise my freedom, but arranging to be able to see you daily by the simple expedient of having you work in my office.'

'Did you particularly ask for me?'

'Of course,' he owned. 'I was attracted to you, just a touch bewitched by you. But naturally I wasn't going to show it. You'd turned me down, remember?'

'I hadn't!' she protested. But, on thinking about it, realised that breaking their date could be seen that way. 'I couldn't ring you—' she tried.

'I know,' he cut in gently, understanding perfectly that

her 'mother complications' were still there. 'So there we are, working in my office, when the green-eyed monster began to appear when your ex-boyfriend Mark reared his ugly head.'

She laughed. Oh, how wonderful—Josh loved her. Oh, he must. She couldn't bear it if it were all a dream. 'Mark's quite good-looking, actually.'

'I didn't really need to know that,' Josh told her nicely, and she laughed again, and he looked as though he delighted to hear her laugh. He went on, 'But no sooner do I hear that Mark has had his marching orders than Stephen is there to plague me.'

'Stephen! Is that why you were so—um—crotchety?'

'I was jealous,' Josh admitted. 'And later annoyed that you refused my second invitation to dinner.'

'That ''I'd better take you for something to eat'' was a dinner invitation?'

'You've remembered?'

'Every word.'

He stilled. 'Like I've remembered, dwelt on, taken out and dissected every word of every sentence you've ever uttered?' he asked quietly.

She swallowed on emotion. It had been like that for him too? She was too full to answer.

'Love me a little?' he asked urgently.

'Yes,' she whispered.

'Darling!' His head came down and he kissed her. Gently she responded, and if she was dreaming then she wanted this wonderful dream to go on and on and on.

Their kiss ended and Josh continued to hold her gently to him. Then, keeping an arm about her, he led her to the sofa. They sat down and he turned to her, to look at her for long, long moments, seeming not to want to say anything more but to just sit looking into her beautiful face.

'Oh, my darling,' he breathed, looking as though he couldn't believe she was not rejecting him. But, perhaps remembering how he had rehearsed and rehearsed everything he did want to say to her if everything did go well, he began, 'So there am I—' but had to break off to give an unrehearsed kiss to the corner of her mouth. 'A man who never asks twice, and most certainly never three times,' he said with a self-deprecating smile, 'wanting to see you again but somehow managing to hold out until Robin and Charlotte's wedding.'

'You knew I'd be there?'

'I made it my business to find out,' he admitted. 'But only to get eaten up with jealousy for my sins when every blasted man at that wedding was after you.'

'Slight exaggeration?' she suggested demurely.

'There weren't many you didn't dance with.'

'I didn't dance with you,' she reminded him.

'I was too busy assuring myself I didn't care who you danced with.'

'You were too busy with the laughing bridesmaid.'

'I—' He broke off, a look of incredulous delight passing over his features. '*You*—were jealous!'

She had to grin. 'Pea-green, if you must know.'

'Darling!' he cried, and kissed her, feasted his eyes on her—and just had to kiss her again. 'I was just doing my best man's duty. Nothing more than that, I promise. Though at the same time I have to admit I was keeping a rather keen eye on what you were getting up to with Greg Williams. Then you went and knocked yourself out—and I knew that night what was wrong with me. That it wasn't just jealousy.'

'It—wasn't?'

He shook his head. 'It was there, battering down the

door of my stubborn refusal to acknowledge it, when I wouldn't allow anyone but the doctor and myself to look after you.' He smiled a tender smile as he told her, 'But I just didn't stand a chance of keeping it at bay any longer as you fell into a natural sleep and I continued to watch you. It was just there. I knew without the smallest doubt that I was in love with this sleeping beauty. I knew I loved you then, and ever would. It was there, and was not going to go away.'

'Oh, Josh!' Erin cried, awe in her voice. But suddenly then she felt able to tell him *her* innermost thoughts, and confessed, 'I knew that night, for all my talk about—um—having more fun, that you were the only man I ever wanted to make love with.'

'You loved me a little then?'

Erin nodded happily. 'I fell a little in love with you that night you sent Gavin home in a taxi.'

Josh stared at her incredulously. 'No!' he denied. 'That was months ago!'

'Months in which that little love has grown to be quite a lot, actually,' she admitted shyly. And absolutely adored him when, murmuring her name, he just had to hold her close and kiss her again and again.

When Josh finally drew back, while still keeping an arm about her, he seemed to have a need to explain why his subsequent behaviour had been as alien to him as it was to her.

'I confess, my love, this new emotion that had crept up on me when I wasn't looking—this deep and all-encompassing love I found I had for you—totally threw me. All I wanted to do was to be with you.'

'But—I didn't see you for over a week after the wedding!'

'Which should tell you what you've done to my confidence.'

Erin stared at him. He was the most supremely confident man she had ever met. 'H-how?' she gasped. 'I...'

'There was I, wanting to see you. In fact at times feeling quite desperate to see you. But I was in love with you, and flattened by that discovery,' he explained. 'My confidence took a pasting, a kind of nervousness setting in as again and again I asked myself—how did you feel about me? You responded to me physically—but that didn't mean you cared for me. You had never phoned me. In all those months since I'd suggested you should, not once had you called my number! I stewed like that for over a week. Then last Monday, after the most emotion-churning weekend I can ever remember, I decided it was no good but that I was going to have to contact you, to see you, to see if I could spot any small glimpse of anything at all remotely like love in your regard for me. But I was booked to fly to New York the next day—would it be better to leave it until I got back. Could I, in fact, wait that long?'

'That was before you saw me with my mother?'

Josh gave Erin a rueful look. 'Oh, it was,' he agreed. 'You weren't supposed to be there. You were supposed to be at your desk in the experimental division. So at first, in that first instant, I thought I'd had you so much on my mind that my imagination was playing tricks on me.' Josh tenderly kissed her before confessing, 'Such an explosion of warmth for you rushed over me when I saw you, I just knew I could not wait until I got back from New York.'

'Then you recognised my companion?'

'Recognised her and, if that wasn't enough to make me see red, there you are bidding each other a fond farewell.'

'You looked murderous!'

'I'm sorry, my darling. Forgive me. But I'd seen my

father with such high hopes, only to see him disbelieving, desolate and near destroyed when Nina Woodward not only turned him down but told him she didn't want to see him again. Not long afterwards he suffered a heart attack.'

'I'm sorry,' she apologised in turn.

'You have nothing to apologise for,' Josh told her lovingly. And, giving her a smile, as though to take the sting out of anything he had said or would say, 'I was blisteringly furious. Nothing would do but that I sorted out a few matters with you before my plane took off the next day.'

'You were still furious when you came here that night,' Erin remembered, without having to search very far in her memory.

'Don't remind me!' he mourned. 'I was downright insulting. When I think of how I treated you... The things I said...'

'Please,' Erin interrupted. He looked so mortified in recalling that time that she couldn't bear it. 'It doesn't matter. Not now. Not now you're here and—'

'It does matter,' Josh cut in. 'You were tearing my heart out. I loved you—yet hated you at the same time because you were doing to me what your mother had done to my father—and I couldn't take it.' Erin kissed him. She just had to. 'Oh, my love,' Josh said throatily. 'I was awake all that night, knowing that not only had I been wrong in what I'd done, in what I'd said, but that I had just blown any slight chance I might have had with you.'

'You did ring from New York to apologise.'

'A fat lot of good that did,' he said, but managed a smile for her. 'Nor was it any better when I came home. There you were, kissing Richard what looked a loving goodbye.'

'He'd just told me that Nina had said no. I felt for him.'

'You would,' Josh said tenderly.

They were lost for a few moments in that time. 'I hit you,' Erin said, still feeling dreadful about that. 'As your behaviour was alien to you, so mine was to me. I'm so, so sorry,' she apologised.

'Don't be—no one deserved it more,' he said with a grin. 'You kissed me better. But just as I'm beginning to find the comfort of holding you, responsive, in my arms, you leave my arms—and only seconds later you're on the phone, making a date with Greg Williams!' Josh sent her another self-deprecating smile. 'A man has his pride, you know.'

'That was why you went all narky!' Erin exclaimed. 'I thought it was because I'd mentioned my mother.'

Josh kissed her. 'You'll—hmm—cancel Thursday's date, I trust?'

Erin laughed. 'With pleasure.'

'And Wednesday's? And who the blazes is Stephen?'

'He works in Experimental. We're friends.'

'And nothing more?'

'Nothing.'

'And if I said I should like to see you Wednesday, and in fact every night this week?'

Her heart started beating erratically again. 'Then naturally I'd be delighted to fit you into my diary.' They kissed, and she just had to say, 'While we're on the subject of jealousy, there was a picture in the paper of you with a lady in New York...'

'You were jealous of...? Fantastic!' Josh exclaimed, truly appreciating that jealousy was not his torment alone. 'Her husband was close by somewhere—they're devoted to each other. I was more interested in getting back to you. In fact couldn't wait to get back to you.

But when everything went pear-shaped between us last night, and my trip to find you in Experimental this morning showed—'

'You went looking for me?'

'It was easy enough to find an excuse. But—did I expect anything else but that you'd had enough and decided to throw your job in? So, unable to see you then, I stewed some more for the rest of the day. But it was only when I started to think about how, only last night, you had said "I used to be a perfectly sane, rational person before I met you" that I began to wonder. Was that the same slightly demented, irrational person I too had become since knowing you? I started to hope.'

'You decided to come over.'

'I wanted to, straight away. But then I stopped to consider how, when I only ever wanted to be pleasant to you, my unannounced visits more often than not ended up being the exact opposite. I thought I'd ring first.'

'You reminded me I owed you a phone call,' she murmured dreamily.

'Waiting for your phone call tonight was one of the most traumatic times I've had to endure,' Josh confessed.

'You knew I'd ring?'

'I'd almost given up hope. Then there you were,' he said, 'and my heart turned over.' He was silent for long moments. And then, looking deeply into her lovely violet eyes, 'Marry me?' he murmured softly.

Erin experienced that drumming in her ears again. 'Yes,' she said, 'I'd like to,' and then quickly got up from the sofa. Oh, heavens, she'd misheard. He hadn't said what she thought he had said. 'I'll—er—make some coffee now, sh-shall I?' she asked, her voice all high and staccato-sounding.

But Josh was there by her side before she had finished.

'I think we'd better make that champagne, don't you, my darling?' he suggested.

'You did s-say what I thought you said?'

'Oh, yes, my love, I did. You once told me, when you shared my bed, that I'd have to marry you. I should have realised then that I was on the way to saying goodbye to my bachelorhood when, to my surprise, the thought of marrying you didn't have me bolting for the door. So, yes, dearest Erin, I did ask you to marry me.'

'You—did?' she questioned shakily, still doubting her hearing.

'Love me?'

'So much.'

Josh took a second or two out to kiss her, and then, looking deeply into her eyes, 'Then, my darling, since I very definitely heard you say yes, you'd like to marry me, I'm afraid I'm going to have to make you honour your promise.' He gave her the tiniest shake. 'All right?' he asked.

Erin, her heart full, nodded. 'Oh, yes. Yes, please,' she answered dreamily, and was held close to his heart for long wonderful seconds before, tenderly, Josh kissed her.

'Now, where, at this time in the morning, can we buy champagne?' Josh asked, looking deep into her eyes.

And Erin stared up at him. She guessed he already knew where; he was that sort of a man. This man, this wonderful man, this man she was going to marry.

He held her close. 'Oh, I do so love you, Erin Tunnicliffe,' he breathed, and just had to kiss her again.

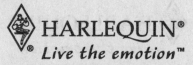

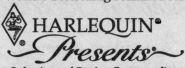

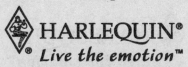

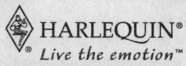

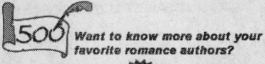

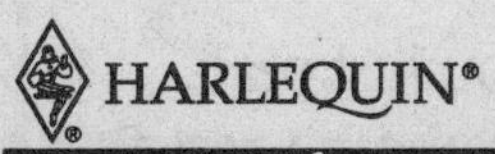

Harlequin Romance®

Coming Next Month

#3791 THE DUKE'S PROPOSAL Sophie Weston
Supermodel Jemima Dare needs to get away from it all. Traveling incognito, she flees to a Caribbean paradise in search of peace. But there's no peace to be found with Niall Blackthorne around! He's aristocratic, irresistible—and a danger to Jemima's heart!

#3792 MISSION: MARRIAGE Hannah Bernard
Lea is turning thirty and the alarm on her biological clock is ringing. But how does a woman with just one ex-boyfriend learn to find Mr. Right? Tom is a serial dater, with no interest in settling down—but he's perfect as a dating consultant! Except their "practice date" leads to more than one "practice kiss."

#3793 THE MAN FROM MADRID Anne Weale
Cally hoped for peace and quiet when she escaped to Valdecarrasca in beautiful rural Spain—but the arrival of mysterious millionaire Nicolás Llorca changed all that!
Nicolás has made it clear he's not looking for long-term commitment...but he's made an offer Cally can't resist!

#3794 A WEDDING AT WINDEROO Barbara Hannay
Piper O'Malley has always come to Gabe for advice. So, after she discovers she's going to lose her home unless she gets married, who better to teach her the art of flirtation? Gabe agrees to give her some tips on how to attract men, but the unexpected chemistry between them takes them both by surprise!